CAPTIVE HEART

A HAWAIIAN CHRISTMAS NOVELLA

OF GOLD & BLOOD
BOOK EIGHT

Jenny Wheeler

Published by Happy Families Ltd

ISBN: 978-0-9951308-7-6 (Paperback)
ISBN: 978-0-9951308-5-2 (Kindle)
ISBN: 978-0-9951308-6-9 (E Book)

OF GOLD & BLOOD SERIES

A`ohe loa i ka hana a ke aloha

Distance is ignored by love.

-Hawaiian Proverb

If you enjoy Captive Heart you may also like a
Free Preview of Ancient Vendetta Book 9.

Details at the end of Captive Heart

One

"Mr. Laurent..." The vibrant, dark-haired Hawaiian he hadn't stopped thinking about since they'd parted months before stood before him, her eyes wide with shock, her dropped bottom lip showing her perfect white teeth.

With a quick indrawn breath, Leilani Manolo lengthened her spine to her formidable five-foot-ten-inch height. Her voice vibrated with accusation as she asked, "What are you doing here?"

Ignoring the wrench in his guts her words provoked, he looked into fierce chocolate-brown eyes. And then his attention hitched on someone behind her. His stomach roiled again. The man who stood at her back placed a proprietorial hand on her shoulder. He was older than Aristide, in a gold braided jacket that announced military authority. But he moved with a younger man's tensile fluidity and his gray-flecked beard whispered seduction, not senility.

Honolulu's spacious Iolani Palace reception hall, where Hawaiian monarch Kamehameha V was hosting a farewell for Benjamin Marshall, the next consul to San Francisco, suddenly felt smaller and hotter.

In one consuming glance, the situation was apparent. Aristide's legs wavered, as if belatedly remembering the ocean roll of the steamboat from which he'd disembarked a few hours ago. Two weeks gazing on pitching, leaden seas, dreaming of this moment, and it came to this. Another man had beaten him to it.

He was making the trip to Honolulu so he and the alluring Miss Leilani Manolo could pick up where they'd left off a few months before in San Francisco, where they'd parted as close, affectionate friends. He secretly hoped for a lot more from their relationship than that.

He'd cradled those dreams to himself as he'd huddled from the wintry winds in the shelter of the lifeboats on deck. Imagined how they'd embrace warmly, talk into the small hours, laugh together. But he saw in an instant there'd be no shared laughter, because Leilani was not pleased to see him.

Her companion closed in. He was at least twenty years older than Aristide, he guessed, which must make him close to fifty, the same age as her despised father, but something about his territorial claim on her arm signaled his interest was not paternal. The planes of his face were lean and smooth, his hazel eyes calculating. The salt-and-pepper beard—mainly salt—did nothing to soften his appearance. He was a loping lone wolf.

"A friend of yours, Leilani? Won't you introduce us?"

Even to a Frenchman, the faint lilt of a European accent heightened his ability to command and intimidate.

Aristide had a sudden conviction he was meeting a Hapsburg count or an Austrian nobleman; an advisor to the king, no doubt.

Leilani gave a barely perceptible shrug, as if the meeting was of small consequence. "I met Mr. Laurent in San Francisco on my last visit, Max."

She turned back to Aristide. "May I introduce Max Moeller, privy councillor and friend of the king. Max, meet Aristide Laurent, a vintner for Sir John Russell in California."

She fumbled with one of the pearl drop earrings she wore, a matching piece to the mother-of-pearl necklace that hung in her draped neckline, as if reassuring herself it was still there.

"I'm surprised to see you here, Mr. Laurent. I thought you'd be busy with your vintage. What brings you to Hawaii?"

She'd adopted a barely perceptible clipped formality. So different from their easy chatter the last time they'd spoken.

She dropped her hand to her skirt. The evening dress wrapped around her shoulders in a sheer green and blue diaphanous flow that nipped into her slender waistline and freed itself again into a marine blue lace skirt. She smoothed the skirt, her hands enclosed in elbow-length sheer gloves. She was trying hard to appear unconcerned, but she was as jumpy as a cat.

Aristide thought back to the first time he'd met this woman, at another semi-formal function, a fund-raising dinner for a charity supported by California Senator Hector de Vile's at San Francisco's Occidental Hotel. Leilani's beguiling openness had him tongue-tied then, too.

Tonight, that fresh candor was nowhere to be seen. He pressed his lips together, cleared his throat. Giving a coherent response took all of his focused willpower.

He reached out a hand to shake Moeller's ham-sized fist. "Mr. Moeller. Very pleased to meet you." He turned to his companion, Honolulu lawyer Titus Cooke.

"If you've been in Honolulu any time at all, I'm sure you will already know my friend Mr. Cooke."

Titus stepped forward and smoothly filled the awkward vacuum.

What am I doing here? Oh, coming to claim your hand. To convince you to return with me to San Francisco. That's all… What do you think?

He cast a hopeless glance to Titus.

Rescue me… Please…

"Aristide and I share common acquaintances," Titus said. "And I finally persuaded him to take a break from wine and come visit while his business is in its quiet season."

"I see. How nice for you."

Max's voice was flat and disinterested as he slid his hand around Leilani's back.

"The king's waiting, my dear," said Moeller. "Please excuse us. Perhaps we'll talk later."

***

Two weeks cooped up in rotten weather on a steamer. Weeks when he could have been readying the vineyard for winter pruning. Instead, he'd chosen to go on a wild goose chase after a woman he couldn't forget.

Aristide resisted the urge to thrust his fingers into his formal collar, to ease the tightness around his throat, and shuffled a few steps further along the slow-moving reception line. Alongside him his new best friend, Titus Cooke, provided a barely audible commentary on local etiquette and the identity of the luminaries who were filling the Iolani Palace, the official reception center for the Hawaiian royal family.

Everyone was queuing to pay their respects to the colossus seated on the carved gilt throne at the far end of the room. The sparkle of gas chandeliers highlighted a sickly sheen on Kamehameha V's face as Titus introduced Aristide and he made a polite bow. The king's eyes were dull, his expression fatigued. As he moved away, Aristide speculated that the throne must have been custom made for the Hawaiian monarch.

"They're sticklers for formal receptions. Something they picked up from the last king's friendship with Prince Albert and Queen Victoria," Titus buzzed in his ear as the crowds spilled in and the surrounding conversation swelled in volume.

"I had no idea," Aristide murmured. "So what's next?"

"The usual thing. A few drinks. Food and speeches. Protestations of commitment and loyalty to king and country."

Titus grinned. "We're sending the new San Francisco consul off to his post with due ceremony. We'll get you an introduction while we're here."

"It's not that different anywhere in the world, is it?" said Aristide. "I wasn't sure what to expect in Hawaii."

Titus nodded, his eyes searching Aristide's face. The vintner had known the barrister-businessman mere hours, since he'd disembarked earlier in the day, but he had a sense Cooke carried a wise head on young—youngish—shoulders. Titus was perhaps ten years older than him, maybe less, but he'd already gained Aristide's confidence as someone he could trust.

"I guess not. But let's find you something to drink. It's hot in here. You're probably parched, and I have the distinct impression that last encounter didn't go as planned."

Two

"Lani? Is that you?"

Malia's melodious voice floated from her Iolani Palace annex bedroom. Her sister was like a skylark who soared high above earthly obstacles, never rushed, always lyrical. Leilani's foot froze in mid-air, noticing too late that her sibling had strategically left her door ajar, anticipating her return.

She'd caught her tiptoeing to bed. Leilani braced herself. She'd hoped to avoid Malia's incisive questioning tonight. Her mind was a confused fog, and she needed a good night's sleep before she faced the affectionate inquisition. How could she have forgotten it was impossible to outwit Malia's super-acute hearing, compensation, she'd long understood, for her partial loss of sight as a complication of childhood measles?

The nervous stomach flutter that had started up the moment she laid eyes on Aristide at the reception stirred deep down inside her. She'd hoped to avoid a post-mortem on tonight's events. Malia was barely a year younger than she, but she seemed to have the wisdom of someone years older.

Please… No soul baring tonight.

She hadn't had time to compose herself, and Malia would see

right through her. Probably understand better than she did what was going on. And she couldn't face that. Not yet, anyway.

"Malia! Sweetheart!! You should have gone to sleep ages ago." She injected all the carefree gaiety she could summon into her words. She'd spent the evening as the special guest of a man many considered a most desirable catch.

Rich, good-looking, debonair… A royal favorite, which wasn't a disadvantage when you were seeking access to plantation water from the king's domains. Yes, he was old enough to be her father, but…

Her father.

She shivered involuntarily as Senator Hector de Vile came to mind. He'd schemed to block her family's sugar exports into California because of an ancient feud with her dead grandfather. What was at the bottom of that, she still didn't know. And then he'd conspired to use her as a hostage in a sinister plot against Aristide's wine company.

She faltered at the half-open doorway, suppressing the memory of the ghastly night when two people died because of de Vile's actions, wanting to glide on to oblivion in her own room next door, yet knowing she must give Malia the satisfaction she sought.

She'd have attended the consul's farewell herself tonight if she hadn't been feverish. She deserved the distraction of a little company.

Malia was sitting up, her back braced by pillows, knees drawn up to her chest. A bedside lamp cast a pale indigo glow on the rich dark hair that tumbled around her shoulders, picking up the bright delight in her smile as she reached to hug Leilani, eyes half-closed and fluttering.

"Tell me all about it. Did you have fun?"

"Fun? Yes. Lots of fun…" Where to start?

"Was Herr Moeller a good escort? Do you like him?"

The corners of her mouth lifted mischievously.

"You know Max hasn't been Herr anything for many years, you

naughty girl," said Leilani with a giggle. "But yes, he was very attentive. Very pleasant company. Lot seemed pleased to see us both. He didn't look well, though."

Prince Lot's—now King Kamehameha V's—doctors worried about his weight and its effect on his overall health. Everyone knew that.

"He doesn't seem to want to do anything about it."

"Is that what's disturbing you?"

"Disturbing me? No. Why?"

"There's something bothering you. I can hear it in your voice…"

A gentle sea breeze blew through the shuttered windows, giving Leilani momentary release from the sense of things closing in around her. The palace sat a few streets back from the dusty waterfront, centered in acres of green parkland.

She so didn't want to talk about tonight until she'd had more time to think. She couldn't bear to recall the flash of misery that had passed over Aristide's face when she'd introduced him to Max.

She'd tried to ignore the sick tremor that unsettled her every time she thought of his shock at seeing her with another man.

What is he thinking? They'd agreed on it. Their destiny is to be apart, and they just have to get on with it.

Malia reached out and gently squeezed her hand.

"What is it, Lani? I won't tell Ani, you know that."

Ani, their *hānai* mother in the Hawaiian way, was old and dying, but her iron determination to rule their lives remained steely to the last. And one of her latest, and it seemed most desperate desires, was to see Leilani married before she departed this earth.

Leilani expelled a lungful of breath she hadn't realized she was holding, and the tightness in her throat eased.

"That friend of mine from San Francisco that I told you about, the Frenchman. He was there."

Malia clapped her hands in delight, stirring a warm violet fragrance in the room as she moved.

"Mr. Laurent? The winemaker?"

"That's him. Aristide Laurent." Even as she spoke his name, her voice broke. Malia wouldn't miss that detail, she knew.

"And you're not happy about it? I thought you liked him…"

Leilani cast her body across Malia's feet, curling up at the bottom of her bed, as if throwing her caution on the evening breeze.

"I did… I do like him," she cried. "Well, I think I do. And that's the problem. He doesn't belong here."

Malia laughed and stroked her head, remaining silent.

Leilani picked herself up, sitting up straight as the words rolled out of her.

"I was awful to him, Malia. I got such a shock to see him. And Max was right there on my elbow. It was the worst moment of my life."

"Why is he here?"

Malia's voice was soft, serious. She wasn't teasing anymore.

"I have no idea. He was with that lawyer, Titus Cooke. Mr. Cooke claimed they were old acquaintances. He said he'd invited him here. I think that's a load of flamdoodle, but we didn't get to talk. Max made sure of that."

"I bet he did."

Her sister's voice had an unusually acerbic edge.

"What do you mean by that?"

"Well, let's face it. It's been clear that Ani, the king, all of them, want to marry you off to Max. It's a dynastic convenience. Lot's never married and not likely to have any kids now. They want to secure the inheritance line, even if the children are only faintly related to the Kamehamehas. And if they amalgamate our lands with Max's it would be a substantial estate allied to the royal house."

When did her young sister develop so much political acumen?

"I didn't know you were interested in politics."

"I'm not, Lani, not really."

Her jaw tightened, the eyes that usually lay half-closed opened wide, and Leilani saw a crinkle of tension in the muscles along her jaw.

"But I care about you. I care about the people I love. That's why I wrote to Kaleo."

"You what?" Lani's heart was fluttering in her throat like the wings of a tiny bird.

"I wrote to Kaleo." The assertiveness of brass took over from the flutes in Malia's musical voice. Kaleo, her twin brother, back in San Francisco.

"I told him what was happening here. What Ani was doing, and how you wanted to do what was right for everyone else so badly, you might forget what was best for you."

Leilani stared. Malia still held her hand, but her touch was no longer gentle and comforting. It was strong and determined. Like the young woman who sat before her, gazing at her with a fierce set to her perfectly proportioned face.

Leilani swallowed hard and choked. Her throat was like sandpaper.

"What... What exactly did you say?"

"I told Kaleo to tell Mr. Laurent that if he ever had any thoughts about a future with you, he'd better get here quick or he'd miss out."

"Arrgh... Malia... How could you?"

She was hot and cold all over, feverish one minute, frozen the next. She put her face into her hands, and tried to catch her breath.

"There's no way..." She gazed at Malia's wandering eyes in despair. "Don't you think we've been over this already...? Gone over it to a painful degree... He can't live here, and I can't live in California... There's nothing we can do. Ohhhh... Why did you interfere? It's going to be a disaster."

Aristide's face came to mind in a momentary recall. She'd snuck a look at him from across the room, and glimpsed the wayward black lock flopping over his right eye, the one she'd teased him about and had so come to love as testimony to his cheerful insouciance… Her chest squeezed at the memory.

We agreed. Our friendship is in the past. I must set my sights on my family's future.

Three

Leilani and Malia had stolen out of the annex at dawn and made for the stables. As they often did, they rode together, Malia's horse roped to Leilani's but with plenty of line for her to gallop along the water's edge, enjoying freedom at the beach she only otherwise found in her music.

By mutual agreement they kept the talk to a minimum, drinking in the glitter of the rising sun on foamy wave crests, listening to the mournful cries of the wheeling seabirds overhead. The pleasant glow of exercise and fresh air engulfed Leilani as they returned their horses to the yard for the boy to groom.

"I'm starving," said Malia. "Race you to the kitchen."

They each dutifully dropped a kiss on Ani's forehead as they flopped into their chairs and took in the breakfast laid out before them.

They were enjoying the benefits of leftovers from last night, that was plain. Raw fish, sweet potato, salmon poke, seaweed snacks, roasted pork shavings and American pancakes, a Malia favorite the cook made especially for her.

"What have you two been up to?" Ani asked in a raspy croak. "And what are your plans for today?"

"Just our usual morning ride," said Leilani. "You know how we both love to get out on the beach…"

Ani nodded, a soft smile on her lips. "You were water babies from when you could walk."

Lani watched as her *hānai* mother—the equivalent of an adoptive mother to foreigners, or the *haole*—sipped her morning coffee. Her left eye was a milky white, evidence of the cataract that was robbing her of her sight. Ani had taken over the care of all the children fostered by their "grandfather," the missionary-entrepreneur Archie Arnold and his wife Cornelia, after Cornelia died.

That family, too, was not of blood but by adoption. All very Hawaiian.

She'd always been there, as Lani and Kaleo's nanny-cum-governess under Cornelia's direction, so they hardly noticed when Cornelia was no longer present. But as the years rolled on, Ani had become a powerful presence, a matriarch with the backing of the royal house, entrusted with raising them for leadership.

Ani lifted her cup to drink, and her hand trembled so much Lani feared she'd slop her coffee. She'd so hate that. She was keenly aware of her own dignity.

Lani glanced away quickly, before Ani saw she'd noticed. Yet another sign the old lady wasn't well. She'd been making dire predictions about dying soon, and Lani worried they weren't only because of her need for control.

She reached for the pancake plate. "Share some of those, you greedy thing." She grinned at Malia to show she was kidding and concentrated hard on squeezing lemon juice on the flat surface and then sprinkling it with sugar.

She caught Ani watching and dipped her head in apology. "I had enough poke last night to satisfy me till Christmas," she joked. "I know you don't approve of *haole* food… but just this once?"

She picked up the rolled pancake, soggy with juice that dripped through her fingers, and bit into it. The sugar crystals crunched delectably under her tongue.

Ani loaded her plate with a small portion of pork and poi.

"You watch your waistline there, girl. In my time big women were highly valued, but those days are long gone. If you want to catch a good husband, you need to stay skinny like the *haole*."

Leilani's insides quivered. In a flash Ani had left her feeling vulnerable.

She rested her elbows on the table, still holding the pancake provocatively close to her mouth.

Here we go again. Back on her hobby horse and I've been in her company less than ten minutes.

"In your time, Ani? That's not so long ago… You're not that old. I'm sure there's lots of good years still to come."

Ani gave one of her characteristic sounds of disapproval, a guttural "Ayee" rumble from deep in her throat. The sound of their childhood. "Not too many more, girl. Not many at all. Speaking of husbands…"

"Which we weren't," Lani said, quick as a flash.

Ani ignored her.

"How was Max Moeller last night?"

"You make it sound like an audition," Lani protested. "We only kept company at a public function. It's hardly a courtship."

"Oh, but it is," Ani said. "And you're not stupid. You well know it."

She set her fork down with an emphatic, impatient clatter. Half the portion she'd taken lay untouched on her plate.

Leilani tried to think back. When did Ani lose her appetite? Was this a new thing, or had it been happening and she hadn't noticed till now?

"Ani, are you feeling all right? You've hardly eaten anything."

Her mother's mouth twisted in frustration.

"I keep telling you, Lani. I'm dying. And I want to see you settled before I go. Then I'll know there'll be someone to take care of Malia too. I want to be sure someone looks after my girls."

Lani gave up on the remnants of her pancake. Suddenly, she didn't feel hungry either.

"I had a very pleasant evening with Mr. Moeller. He was a considerate and interesting companion. But I don't see why we have to rush things. We've got plenty of time…"

"No Leilani, we don't. It's not just my health. The king wants things settled too. You know he's not well. He's probably in worse health than I am. And Lot wants to see you and Max betrothed. It's as simple as that. He knows he'll never have children. He hasn't named a successor. And he doesn't want to leave a vacuum. That could cause trouble." She pushed her plate away.

"He wants you betrothed by Christmas. Your mother may not have had the strongest of bloodlines, but your father Matthew Lilolilo was a recognized Kamehameha descendant. Distant, I know. But still better than most of the others on offer. And Max is a steady pair of hands. A very rich, steady pair of hands. It's an ideal match."

"Christmas!" Lani's breath caught in her throat. She had an awful sense of her freedom, her joie de vivre, draining away into dusty duty. "But I've got too much to do to get engaged by Christmas!"

Ani studied her, a stern, impassive presence. Like one of those Easter Island statues, a staunch block of carved stone.

"Like what? What's more important than preserving the stability of the throne?"

"Well, like settling the water rights issue on Maui, for one. We can't expand sugar production without more water. We need that water by the next growing season, and we can't start digging the irrigation channels until we know what's happening. I don't know why Lot is taking so long to decide."

Ever since she'd been back from San Francisco, Lani had been laying the platform for a big expansion in their sugar business, but they needed extra water to do it. Lot had the water and his land was right next door to theirs, but he was dithering over sharing the rights.

Ani shook her head. Her sound eye was a sharp black bead that pierced Lani's composure.

"There will be no water without Max. Don't you understand? Lot needs to keep both of you happy. He can't have one of you dissatisfied. When your lands unite in marriage—that's when you'll get the water. As far as I understand it, anyway. No marriage, no water."

She pushed back from the table with a triumphant thrust.

"I'm surprised it's taken you this long to realize it. If you want the water, Lani, you must take the man."

Four

"Max Moeller? You're up against the big guns there, Aristide. No getting around it."

Aristide studied Titus Cooke's lean, intelligent face as his new friend put another fork load of bacon and egg pie in his mouth and chewed appreciatively.

He was fortunate to have someone like Cooke to give him a fast introduction to Hawaii. It would take him months on his own to collect the valuable information that flowed with Titus's every observation. The man knew everyone who was anyone and many more besides. He was a respected local identity, Hawaiian born, who'd done an internship in his grandfather's Boston law firm. When he felt ready, about ten years ago, he'd returned to his homeland to set up one of the most highly regarded practices in the capital.

His introduction to Titus had come thanks to Leilani Manolo's twin, Kaleo, who'd remained in San Francisco as an import agent when his sister returned home. He understood there was a lot she needed to do here—to supervise the manufacturing and dispatch of their sugar and care for an elderly relative.

He couldn't deny the instant attraction he'd felt on their first meeting, and they'd become close friends. But life was taking them in opposite directions. They both knew it, and they'd agreed there wasn't anything they could do about it.

The warm intimacy they'd shared when they were together in San Francisco was difficult to maintain in their letters, especially when they had no plans to meet again. Aristide had tried to accept that was how it had to be. He really had.

But when he'd seen Kaleo at the Pike Consulting offices one afternoon on a visit to arrange a shipment of their wine to New York, Leilani's brother hinted that if he dreamed of ever sharing a future with his sister, he needed to act now. Their younger sister Malia was concerned that Lani was being put under a lot of pressure from the court, although she was vague on the details. Aristide didn't wait for another warning.

He'd asked for special leave from his employer, Sir John Russell, the owner of Vino d'Oro. Luckily, it was the quiet time for the vineyard. Russell had given him six weeks—until late January—to sort things out, and he'd jumped on the next available steamboat.

According to Kaleo, Manolo Sugar was in competition for water rights, and Kaleo worried his sister would put family interests ahead of personal ones.

"If you've got any secret hopes of being with Lani, ever, you need to go see her." Kaleo had given him a hard look and then broken into a cheeky grin. "She mightn't thank you for it, but you'll never know if you don't try."

***

A light breeze stirred the fronds of the coconut palms that fringed the shore, producing a relaxing sighing sound. Peals of laughter and the raised voices of young men and children out on the beach—some chancing the waves—carried to where Aristide and Titus sat, basking in warm winter sun. The picnic lunch they were sharing in the lawyer's beachfront garden would have been magical if Aristide didn't feel so miserable.

Over his host's shoulder, white sand stretched to the water's edge where the waves surged and retreated soothingly. Aristide stretched his legs in front of him and tried to ignore the heaviness that pressed down on him.

Titus swallowed and reached for his coffee. "He's a major landowner, with estates on several islands. Sugar plantations on Maui and Kauai. Cattle ranching on the Big Island. I believe he's also got considerable Honolulu real estate. And he's influential. He's on the king's council and has a big say on what goes on. His opinion counts."

"I see. And no scandals? No wife hidden away he's not owning up to? No secret gambling?"

Titus laughed.

"You wish."

His penetrating blue-gray eyes sharpened.

"Although there are rumors he's made his climb to power on the backs of his council colleagues. Ezra Chance, for example, the minister of the interior. Ezra likes to gamble and doesn't know when to stop."

Aristide's interest quickened.

"What are you talking about?"

"Insiders say Moeller's made big loans to the minister, to help him meet his gambling debts. That's why he always seems to get what he wants. Ezra can't deny him, or he might pull the loan."

"Sounds like I'm completely outclassed." Aristide gave a rueful laugh. "Maybe I'm finally getting what I deserve."

"Why do you say that?"

Titus finished eating and reached for the coffeepot, refilling both their cups.

"I guess Leilani is the first woman I've ever wanted to spend the rest of my life with. I've never understood that urge before now. But seeing Leilani with Max the other night… It made me realize what we had is worth fighting for."

Titus gave him a wry grin.

"If it's that important to you, it's a good thing you've come now."

"Why do you say that?"

Titus shrugged. "There are rumors Max and the Manolo family are in competition for the same resource—water from the king's Maui domain. In Hawaii, we always want to keep everyone happy. I imagine there's a high-stakes negotiation going on in the king's private chambers."

Aristide considered Titus's words, picking at the grass restlessly as he turned them over in his mind.

"So you're saying Max is a big sugar man? Because of course Leilani's family is in sugar. That's why she had to come back here."

Titus turned his chair to face the beach and settled himself again.

"They're about the same size. They're two of the biggest sugar producers in the kingdom. But Moeller's got a lot of other collateral as well. He's a shareholder in Diamond Sugar—the super agency which deals with sugar exports. They've got a monopoly since they bought out their biggest competitor a few months back."

Aristide nodded. "Leilani has talked about Diamond. I don't think she particularly liked them. Quite the opposite."

Titus continued. "Diamond owns the shipping line which carries most Hawaiian sugar to market, and a sugar refinery in San Francisco. Hawaiian sugar is dominated by Diamond and Max Moeller. Lani's family has a lot of land, but Max controls the export agents, shipping and refining."

"Great. Lani sure knows how to pick 'em."

"Don't give up just yet, Aristide. We'll see what else we can dig up."

Five

"I need you to do this for me, Ezra. You owe me…"

Max Moeller leaned over the billiards table in the palace's private lounge and lined up his shot. The white ball made a satisfying hollow-sounding *thunk* as it sent the target spinning into the corner pocket, tapping and carrying a second ball with it. Two sunk in one stroke.

He gave a triumphant shout. He was on a roll.

Ezra Chance, Hawaiian minister of the interior and ex officio member of the House of Nobles and Privy Council, frowned and shook his head.

"Pure luck," he said. "Bet you can't repeat it."

"You should know better than to bet against me, Ezra." Max stepped away from the green baize-covered table and reached for the blue chalk. "Magic" chalk, pool buffs called it. As he anointed his cue, he surveyed his options.

"What will you bet with? Forgive me for pointing out you can't afford the cash. You've got none. So how about…" He lounged against the table edge, taking pleasure in riling his friend's sensitivity.

Chance was a powerfully built man, still in excellent form for his years, erect in posture, broad across the shoulders, with a strong face and carefully trimmed beard. The very picture of a senior royal advisor. But Max knew a bluff when he saw one. He noted the slick sheen at Ezra's temples, the ripple of sweat down the side of his face. Ezra's eyes didn't leave his face.

"What?" he said. "What do you want now?"

"Come, come, Ezra. Don't be like that. You don't want me to pull the float, do you?"

Chance ignored the implications.

"What do you want?" He spoke testily.

"Just a little push getting this water business completed, that's all. The king's taking a dastardly long time to approve something that should be routine. Diamond Sugar is the biggest grower in the realm. I'm his more-than-loyal subject and close neighbor. It shouldn't be taking this long for him to make up his mind."

"You talk like you're the only fish in the sea." Chance's deep bass sounded peevish.

"I'm the most obvious. The one who can do the most for him."

"I wouldn't forget that blood runs thicker than water," Ezra replied.

Max's fingers on the slender cue stiffened.

"I presume you're referring to the Manolos' claim. The beautiful Leilani and her brother?"

"Who else?" said Chance.

"There's no need for her to miss out. You know that."

"Oh? So, the king gives Diamond the water and then you generously agree to share it with the lovely young lady… Is that how it goes?"

"Why not? Seems perfectly reasonable to me."

"But not to Lot, most likely. He doesn't like to disappoint family."

Moeller's face reddened.

"Are you in or out?" he snapped.

Chance shrugged. "I don't have much choice, do I?"

Max Moeller's face relaxed, and his straight white teeth flashed in a relieved smile.

"Glad you see it that way, my friend. Very sensible of you."

He flexed his shoulders to relax his arms and leaned back over the table.

He took a concentrated minute to line up his target.

Then his shooting arm made a sinuous, controlled thrust. The red and white clicked together, and followed one another into the netted corner, leaving the black as the last easy shot.

He grinned at Ezra. "Told you not to bet against me."

They heard the tap of heels in the hallway.

The king's chamberlain David Kinau put his head around the door, checking the scene.

"Oh. It's just you two. Pardon me for interrupting."

A dark feminine head looked over his shoulder.

"Oh. Mr. Moeller. I didn't expect to see you here."

Leilani Manolo was wearing a tangerine dress with a brightly patterned bodice which combined Pacific and American style in one satisfying garment. Fresh, original, but nicely modulated. Coral earrings and necklace completed the ensemble.

"Nor I you, Leilani. What brings you to the king's quarters at this hour?"

David Kinau spoke up. "His Majesty needs cheering up. His gout has been giving him what-ho. So he's invited Miss Manolo to come and sing for him. You know how he enjoys hearing the old songs."

There was a long pause. Max Moeller laid down his cue and picked up the jacket he'd discarded when he'd started the game.

"You'll charm him, I'm sure." It was said with a hint of tartness.

Leilani glanced at the chamberlain, unsure if they expected a reply.

"Have a pleasant evening." Ezra's voice carried a warmth Max's had conspicuously lacked.

And Max could see by the sharp look the Manolo girl flashed his way that she hadn't missed his sour note.

She was a beautiful woman, no doubt about it. Endowed with acres of inherited land, too. However, he wasn't going to stand aside and allow her to entice Lot into a special water deal that excluded him, no matter how charming her musical performance. He knew from intimate experience. Trust no one.

Six

Ezra Chance tapped his billiard cue on the leather-trimmed table edge.

"What was all that about? Gone sour on her? What's wrong with her? She looks like an angel."

"I'm getting fed up with waiting, that's all. Lot says it's all but signed and sealed, so I don't know why we're facing these confounded delays."

"The filly doesn't see you as an irresistible option? Is that it? Your feelings injured?"

It was Ezra's opportunity to bait his friend.

"It's not a matter of injured anything. It's a simple matter of business. A bonus deal. She gets me *and* the water. And the king gets babies in his bloodline. Fresh stock, so to speak, offspring who might one day inherit. Probably long after Lot's gone, but that's not my problem. What's so difficult about that?"

Ezra raised a derisive eyebrow.

"Heaven forbid that the gal should make a play for sole rights. She's got an 'in' with his Royal Highness if she's singing him lullabies. What would you do then?"

"I'd put the squeeze so hard on you, you'd hardly be able to breathe," said Moeller. "I'm not playing, Ezra. I am going to get that damned water. And you're going to see I do."

"Aren't you guilty of playing both sides against the middle?"

"What do you mean?"

"That American party girl who's in town—what's her name? Honeybun? The Cleveland heiress. You're spending a lot of time with her when you're not squiring Miss Manolo about town. Don't think it hasn't been noticed."

Max's jaw clamped shut, his face reddened.

"Don't be ridiculous. She's the daughter of a close business colleague. Of course I make sure she's looked after. Gerald Cleveland would have my guts for garters if anything happened to her while she was here."

"Looks to me more like the old man has sent her over here to buy himself some time," said Ezra Chance.

Hot blood pulsed at Max's temples.

"What are you talking about?"

"I know you've got Gerald Cleveland in the same headlock as me. You own most of Diamond Sugar because of the money he owes you for his gambling debts. The world might think they're still rich, but you and me know he's borrowed against most of his other assets.

"He's built the Cleveland empire on sand, and it's about to come crashing down. Honeybun looks like a sacrificial lamb, if you ask me. I almost feel sorry for her."

"Her name is not Honeybun. And 'sacrificial lamb'?" Max's voice was scornful. "Spare me the melodrama. She's a remarkably worldly twenty-three-year-old who knows what has to happen if she's to be left with any independent means at all. And from what she's said, she has no intention of letting her father burn down the house."

Seven

The king had kept Leilani up deep into the night, reminiscing about old times and requesting song after song, so Leilani slept in and she and Malia delayed their ride until after breakfast. Leilani had her own reasons for wanting to ride later, so the king's insomnia provided a perfect excuse.

She'd woken punching the pillow, dreaming of fighting her way out of a low hanging fog. As she blinked at sunlight pouring in through the un-shuttered windows, she decided she wasn't just suffering from a lack of sleep. The king's somber mood had left her feeling under a cloud.

Kamehameha V was turning forty-one next week, and he'd announced with the certainty of a man able to command his subjects to do whatever he wished that he wanted Leilani to sing for him again on his birthday. "You never know, it might be my last."

She'd placed her music on the piano stand and lit into a cheerful Stephen Foster classic.

When she finished, Lot responded with delighted clapping. "I missed you when you were away," he said with a twinkle in his eye. "You're an essential fixture around here. You lighten up the dull old dutiful day."

She smiled and said teasingly, "The burdens of office don't weigh too heavily, do they, Lot? You've got good men around you."

"That I have, Leilani. But I miss Lilolilo."

The king's brother, Alexander Lilolilo Iolani, had reigned with his wife Queen Emma as Kamehameha IV. He'd died nearly a decade before, but the brothers had been inseparable when younger and Lot had no wife, no family, to fill his home with love and laughter.

He'd renamed the royal house as Iolani Palace in memory of Kamehameha IV, because one of his brother's middle names—Io—signified the royal hawk.

Kamehameha V and his widowed sister-in-law, the Dowager Queen Emma, were bosom pals. Rumor had it he'd delicately sounded her out about a prospective marriage between them, but she'd diplomatically rejected the approach.

"Don't leave marriage too late, Leilani. We Kamehamehas haven't fulfilled our duties in that respect. No *mo'opuna* to carry the work into the next generation. When I go, I don't know who will take over."

"Oh, your Royal Highness, that's a long way off. Anything could happen..."

Lot shook his head slowly and sadly. "Probably not, Leilani. Probably not..."

***

As they walked their horses over the sand, Leilani told Malia about the night before.

"It's sad, Bubs," she said, using the twin's old childhood endearment for their younger sibling.

"He's not in good health, and he hears the bell tolling. Even hinted his birthday next week might be his last. And he seems preoccupied with the succession. Who it might be, I mean."

Malia said nothing, but her face reflected a keen alertness that belied her shadowed eyes. When you tuned in to Malia, you understood she was wholly present in the moment, alive to everything going on around her. Only fools passed her over as the invisible "blind girl," though Leilani knew there were plenty who did.

Malia's two dogs, Kāne and Kū, named after the Hawaiian gods of fertility and war, trailed behind the sisters, half-heartedly chasing seagulls they didn't expect to catch, wet, red tongues lolling in the morning sun.

Malia turned in a semicircle, following the sound of their pounding paws and excited yelps, her face radiant with smiles. They were ugly but loving Honolulu "poi" dogs, fat-bodied and short-legged, short-haired and with the breed's unusual flattened head, said to result from eating too much poi. Kāne had one blind eye—the result of an infection when he was a pup—and was the standard brown color, typical of the dogs their ancestors had bred for food.

Kū, on the other hand, was a spotty gray and white. He was younger and spent a lot of time chasing flies for entertainment. Both were dim-witted and somewhat sluggish, as was the poi dog nature, though they got excited over beach outings.

"Let's mount and have a gallop," Malia called, foot in her stirrup. "The dogs need a blast and so do we. Come on. A good airing in the sea breeze will blow away last night's sad talk."

"Suits me," said Leilani, as she followed Malia to mount. "Race you to the big rock."

***

As Aristide sat outside with Titus on his third day in Hawaii, he marvelled at how quickly his San Francisco memories merged with Pacific sounds and smells—starting with the appetite-enhancing pineapple fragrance wafting from the fresh fruit breakfast laid out in the warm winter sun.

He let his eyes roam down to the waterline. Golden-skinned men with powerfully sculpted bodies disappeared into the white surf, their torsos glinting as the sun caught the sea spray on their broad muscled shoulders.

Titus had explained how in Hawaiian history, excelling at wave sliding was essential for spiritual and physical dominance. Chiefs competed in surfing games because they involved spiritual force, knowledge of the ocean, physical engagement and beauty, all considered essential attributes for holding power.

The cheerful taunts and challenges that carried up the beach from the shore pulsed with a friendly rivalry that showed nothing much had changed in the two hundred years since tribal warfare had ceased.

"This is another world," he said, turning to Titus. "When I met Kaleo and Lani, I didn't have a clue about all this. San Francisco must have seemed strange to them, but they didn't show it for one minute."

Titus grinned. "It's good you're here. What do you want to do today?"

Titus had been acting as his personal guide, introducing him around at the consul's farewell, and yesterday taking him on a general tour of Oahu, pointing out landmarks along the way.

He'd been generous with his time, but Aristide knew Titus needed to work, and he didn't want to become a burden.

"That newly appointed consul is leaving later today. Thought I might call on him and have a more detailed chat—offer my services to him as a guide to San Francisco, as you've done for me. It might help me understand the challenges he faces, too."

He didn't say it might also help him understand the barriers Leilani faced in the sugar business.

Every time he recalled her cool dismissal, his stomach knotted. He'd traveled two thousand miles in a stinky tub to see her, and she couldn't give him the time of day.

Titus pushed a plate of chopped pineapple toward him.

"I have to decide how long I'm staying," Aristide said. "I might wander around the port and see what ships are sailing for San Francisco in the next month. I've got nothing booked yet."

"You're not planning on leaving already?" Titus's mouth turned down in a disappointed moue. "You've only just got here."

"It was always just going to be a holiday, Titus. Sir John wants me back by the end of January. That means I need to be on board something by mid-January at the latest. But if there's a suitable ship leaving earlier, I'm tempted to take it. I've still got plenty of time to see Hawaii."

Titus tapped his fingers on the table, considering.

"It rather depends on whether Leilani Manolo softens her attitude, doesn't it? I know you've not talked about it, but her reaction the other night was disappointing." He looked up with a challenge in his smoky eyes. "I thought it was, anyway."

Aristide shrugged. "I suppose. But you know, I hadn't thought it through properly. I didn't expect to be seeing her like that, at a formal function the night I arrived, and with another man. Probably not the best circumstances for anyone."

He turned away and resumed his pose of casual indifference, gazing out to sea.

Titus followed the line of his sight, and his relaxed body straightened.

"Speaking of which … Well, I'll be blowed."

He jumped to his feet. But Aristide had already spotted the distinctive sway-bottomed silhouette of two dogs, galloping up the beach ahead of two women leading horses. Titus had pointed them out in the distance yesterday, racing up the beach behind the same two horses. He'd know them anywhere.

***

Leilani's skin was tingling as she approached the row of coconut palms that fringed Titus Cooke's property. All that sea breeze and spray she'd just been in, she told herself. Nothing at all to do with the man she was about to meet again.

Her blood surged with triumphant satisfaction as she reached out to return Cooke's welcoming handshake. She'd shamefully longed for this exchange ever since she'd been standoffish with Aristide two nights ago.

And after seeing Max Moeller's swagger and the king's downcast mood last night… a deep uneasiness about getting caught up in palace power games overwhelmed her. She needed to see Aristide to remind her of "real life," whatever that was.

Back in San Francisco in the winter, he'd listened patiently as she'd brooded over the events that led to the deaths of her dear friends, Cyrus and Misty May. Could she have done anything to prevent that cataclysm? Aristide hadn't made light of her soul searching, but he'd helped her set it aside and laugh, too.

"Leilani… Malia… so good to see you. Enjoying a little light exercise, are you?"

Titus Cooke's eyes offered Leilani an unspoken challenge, but softened to a marked tenderness as he turned to Malia.

He took a step toward her and her dogs sniffed around his legs and then relaxed, satisfied he presented no threat.

Malia smiled and offered her hand.

"Titus. Good to see you too."

He touched her elbow with the subtlest of hints, directing her to a bench seat a few feet away from the breakfast table. They stood looking at one another for a few more seconds, sharing a common understanding; they didn't want to intrude on the reunion that was taking place in front of them. Then Malia took Titus's arm and allowed him to guide her back to the bench.

***

He'd forgotten how tall she was. As Aristide rose to meet Leilani her physical presence was momentarily breathtaking. He'd also blanked out how irresistible she was at close quarters.

Fresh and radiant from her ride, and as natural and sparkling as the sea spray that dampened her dark hair, he was for the third time in their short acquaintance tongue-tied as he gazed into her face.

By all the saints! Why did she affect him this way? Offering his hand in a formal shake felt all wrong too, so he stood mute and motionless as she hesitated before him.

He gestured to Titus's empty chair and sat down himself. He drew in a deep breath and found his voice.

"Why hello, Leilani. Another surprise. I thought you had far too much important business to bother with us."

His voice had a sharpness he hadn't intended, and he hated it.

She impulsively reached across the table to touch his hand, but halted halfway and then drew back again, distrusting the gesture. He grinned to himself. She'd made exactly the same warm gesture of companionship the first time he'd met her, at the fateful dinner with Bully Pike before the man's unfortunate death later the same night. They'd been too far apart that night for her to reach him.

Aristide's eyes flicked from her hand to her face. She gave her lips a quick nervous lick, but her jaw was resolute, her eyes steady and determined.

"Aristide, I have to apologize for the other night. I was so rude… I want to explain. Your arrival was just so unexpected…"

She gave her lips another quick, unconscious lick.

"Seeing you, I mean. It was the last thing… and I've had so much going on… But I know that's no excuse. I was a coward."

He shook his head, drinking in the soft chime of her voice, the apologetic cast in her eyes, the graceful tilt of her head.

"Don't, Leilani. Don't torture yourself. My fault entirely. After all, didn't you tell me once you didn't like surprises? I should have remembered."

He gave her a cheeky grin, as if the snub had been the merest misfire, and then reached out and gave her hand a gentle, consoling squeeze. He released it immediately.

"And yes, I could see you've got a lot going on…"

Her eyes flashed.

"You said… We agreed…" She cast her head around wildly, taking in that Titus and Malia had distanced themselves from this conversation, and she stood.

"Can we walk? Like we did that last day on the Pacific Coast? I feel as if I'm going to burst if I don't move…"

Aristide stood abruptly. The cups rattled on the table as they got up.

As they exited through the beach gate, Titus and Malia stood.

"You two going for a walk? That sounds like a lovely idea. I'll show Malia around the garden. We'll see you soon."

Eight

"I'm scared, Aristide. I feel like people are scheming behind my back. Even my beloved Ani. She thinks she knows better than I do what's good for me."

Lani kicked at the sand in front of her with her bare foot.

"I'm a pawn in palace games. Trouble is, I hardly know myself anymore."

She glanced up at him with wide, troubled eyes.

There was nothing he'd have liked more than to take her into his arms and comfort her.

But he understood he'd do irreparable harm if he even attempted it.

Hawaiian society might seem free and casual, but Aristide recognized within hours of his arrival that a strong decorum underlaid everything pertaining to the court. And as one of the king's familiars, linked by bloodlines, however hazy, Lani had to observe the expected conventions.

Society had already acknowledged she was being wooed by a powerful man at court, one with the king's endorsement. It would be a royal insult to ignore or intervene.

"I guess all you can do is bide your time while you sort it out," said Aristide. He shook his head in mock dismay.

"That sounds weak, doesn't it? Old age is getting to me."

They tramped a good stretch of the beach, suitably distanced, never touching, as they caught up on what each had been doing since they'd last been together. A quiet wariness replaced their earlier frank openness, as they acknowledged the things that must be left unsaid.

At least Aristide assumed Leilani saw it the same way he did. He wasn't going to ask.

His heart pounded whenever he caught her eye, so he made himself adept at talking while walking, looking straight ahead as if reveling in the open sky, the swaying palms. Anything not to gaze into her face and see what he was missing. Until he couldn't avoid it any longer.

They were trailing their way back to Titus's house. Aristide had followed Leilani's lead and taken off his boots and rolled up his trousers. He carried the shoes in one hand and splashed his bare feet through the sizzling incoming waves as they dawdled.

Leilani had laid out for him the dilemma shaping up at court; the king reluctant to show a preference for one of his prominent subjects over another. Her breakfast conversation with Ani about the water rights offered as a package deal, along with her agreement to marrying Moeller.

"I don't know how we got to this point," she said, semi-despairing. "I was so confident Lot would give us the water. I mean, we're right next door, we're related, and he's always considered Ani's extended family."

She jumped over the crest of the wave that was rolling in deeper than the others.

"Anyway," she said, turning shyly toward him. "Enough about me. Tell me about you. And what possessed you to come here?"

Her eyes fixed on him, dancing with mischief. The little minx was enjoying embarrassing him.

He took a deep breath. His Adam's apple seemed to lodge in his throat, making swallowing suddenly difficult.

"What possessed me to come to Hawaii?" He was buying time as his eyes dropped from her face to her long, lean body.

She wore another of the flowing traditional gowns, the muumuu, but she'd cut it shorter than was usual so it barely reached to her knees, giving plenty of leeway to walk the shoreline, and keep dry, he guessed. The cotton fabric was a swirling mix of turquoise and emerald green with splashes of yellow.

"Like the dress," he said. "Did you get it here?"

She pushed his chest with a playful gesture and then jumped back out of reach.

"Don't avoid the question," she laughed. "Why did you come here?"

"You just want to hear me say it, don't you?" Aristide groaned. "I came here, my dear Miss Manolo, because your brother said I should."

She looked momentarily outraged.

Is that mock shock? She already knows this. She's playing me.

"My brother? Kaleo? And you needed someone to tell you to do it?" She gave a teasing laugh.

He stopped walking, ignored the knee-deep water that hit the backs of his calves and drenched his trousers.

"You know why I came here, Leilani. I've thought of you every day since I left you at Elizabeth Westerhoven's on that last night. I've asked myself again and again what we could have done differently."

He moved out of the wave line as another surge of cool water hit him.

"When Kaleo told me if I ever wanted you in my life again, I needed to come now, I knew I had to do it."

He gave a huge sad sigh and gazed at her, all pretense gone.

"Trouble is, I still don't have any answers about how it can happen. Even if we… even if you… wanted it to."

Nine

"Coo-ee. Anyone home?"

Leilani Manolo stepped onto Titus Cooke's well-kept front lawn and paused, listening for her sister's answering cry. Their horses were happily grazing, still tied on long leads to the palms at the gate. The dogs dozed in the shade of the table but jumped up, tails wagging, at the sound of her voice.

Malia was still here somewhere or the animals wouldn't be here. She heard faint strains of music from inside, and she turned to Aristide, who was treading silently in her footsteps.

"Sounds like they're at the piano."

As she pushed down the hall toward what she assumed was the parlor, the music stopped and she heard Malia's gurgling laughter.

The light was dim after the bright sunshine outside, but Leilani could make out two people seated at a handsome ebony piano. Malia and Titus were side by side on a piano bench, hands outstretched on the keys, playing duets. Another couple, a young blonde woman and a much older man, watched from a settee.

"Max. What are you doing here?"

The words were out before she'd stopped to think about how they'd sound. He looked up with a pinched twist to his mouth.

"I dare say I could ask you the same thing," he said, flicking a significant look at Aristide, and making no attempt to get up and greet her.

Again, that sour note, the same derisive edge she'd detected last night.

What is it with this man?

Titus spun off the piano stool and stood.

"Oh good. You're back." He hesitated, his face flushing. "Leilani, you know Max of course, but I'm not sure if you've met Honey Cleveland. She's an old family friend of my father's from the States. Honey, meet Miss Leilani Manolo."

Titus paused, his normally smooth composure ruffled.

"Aristide, I believe you and Honey met the other night, didn't you?"

Honey bounced up from the settee arm where she'd perched, peering over Malia's shoulder.

She flicked a slight nod, a cool smile, in Leilani's direction.

"Honey Bancroft Cleveland. My mother was a Bancroft. My father is Gerald Cleveland. The Bancrofts and Clevelands of Diamond Sugar. We've a long history in the business, as I'm sure you'd know."

Leilani struggled to mask her surprise. She'd heard talk someone from the Diamond Sugar family was in town, but she hadn't been aware she was so young, and so pretty.

"Oh, I see. Nice to meet you." She was about to inquire if that was how she and Max knew one another when Honey stretched out her hand, beaming at Aristide.

"Mr. Laurent. How delightful to meet up with you again. Have you been enjoying your stay in Honolulu?"

Leilani raised an eyebrow to Titus, who acknowledged her mute comment with the briefest of shrugs. Before Aristide had time to do anything other than shake Honey's hand, Titus spoke.

"Honey arrived ten days or so ago. Her father has arranged for her to get to know more about the family business here. She was interested—and it keeps her out of trouble."

Titus's weak grin didn't conceal that his jest dropped like a stone, and Malia came to the rescue.

"Did you enjoy your walk, Lani? Titus and I have been having such fun playing terrible music."

Her head turned toward the lawyer and she laughed again, a soft husky snicker that told Leilani she was completely at home in his company.

Max was still regarding her with a disgruntled expression.

"Yes, we had a good catch up on the San Francisco news. I got the lowdown on what our brother's been up to, for a start."

Involuntarily her eyes flicked to Aristide, but he was gazing out the window.

Honey stepped in close to him, and he acknowledged her presence with a smile. "Miss Cleveland. How are you enjoying Honolulu?"

She swung her hips in a girly gyration which was simultaneously coy and flirty.

Leilani suppressed a shudder.

"Oh, I am having the most wonderful time. Titus and Max have been wonderful. They've been taking such good care of me. I want to repay their kindness by holding a little soiree later this week, and you must come. It'll be such fun."

Leilani couldn't think of anything she'd enjoy less. Now she recalled Max had mentioned the girl in passing, but she hadn't realized they were such cozy pals.

Honey swung back to claim Max's attention and Aristide shot Leilani a down-at-the-mouth grimace.

What can I do?

But his eyes twinkled dangerously.

Lani made a move toward the door. "I really had better be going, Titus." She looked to her sister. "Are you happy to come now, Malia, or will you stay?"

Malia gave Titus a brief smile. "Thanks so much for your hospitality today, Mr. Cooke. I had fun."

"Anytime," Titus said through a grin. "And please, it's Titus. As long as you can put up with my awful playing, that is."

Malia gave another chuckle.

Ten

"Can you believe that woman?"

They were wending their way back home, leading their horses up the dusty street from the port to Iolani Palace.

And Leilani had fizzed with indignation the whole way.

"Honey *Bancroft* Cleveland… We've got a long history in sugar, as I'm sure you'd know."

She mimicked the Boston beauty's simpering tone, exaggerating for effect.

Malia laughed.

"She seems to know how to lead men around by the nose…" She giggled again.

"She has Max and Titus—and after today, probably Aristide too—on a string as much as we do these nags here." She stroked her horse's neck and grinned again.

Leilani stared at her stonily. She'd barely given Max a thought when he wasn't with her. That wasn't good, was it? Surely if she cared about him, she'd take more notice.

"What? Not funny, Sis? She's really got under your skin, hasn't she? What's the problem? She's just a silly girl. There's plenty around town like her, and I've never seen you mind before."

Leilani didn't want to admit that Malia had a point. What was the problem?

She considered the question. Had Honey made her feel a fool for not noticing her sooner?

Was it because she'd annoyed Max by going walking with Aristide, and she didn't want to face up to what his displeasure might mean?

Or was it because Honey Cleveland reminded her so much of that woman in San Francisco, Candy Meadows, that old girlfriend of Aristides' who'd come close to destroying them both with her malicious lies?

She produced a third option for Malia. One that was easier to admit to.

"Perhaps I'm just jealous someone can pull favors from family connections while we have to pretty well fend for ourselves. She swans in here and sets herself up, all sweetness and light, and the men fall at her feet. While any connections we might have don't seem to be working all that well for us right now."

Her sister watched her with that glowing combination of fierce intelligence and piercing intuition that was pure Malia.

The corners of her lips lifted in a wry smile.

"Could be." She allowed for a calculated pause. "But don't you think it's simpler than that? Maybe you just don't like the thought of her getting her claws into Aristide."

It was a statement. Not a question.

Leilani's jaw dropped.

"Of course not," she snapped. "I was the one who walked away the other night, wasn't I?"

But even as the blood rushed to her temples in angry denial, a sinking feeling in her stomach told her Malia had hit gold again.

Her sister had guessed her truth before she was even willing to acknowledge it herself.

She mightn't be able to have Aristide Laurent herself, but that didn't mean she liked the idea of him carrying on with his life without her. Especially if it meant having a featherhead like Honey Bancroft Cleveland at his side.

Eleven

"What do you mean, Lot says he wants a betrothal announced by the weekend? What are you talking about?"

Leilani leaned on the bare wood of the kitchen table with both hands flat on the hard surface. Vice-like pain drilled at her temples and her mouth was furry.

She glared at Ani across the breakfast dishes. Ani glowered straight back, her eyes unrepentant black coals in her wrinkle-gouged dark face.

"Don't act all surprised, Leilani." Her voice sounded like a rusty, dried-up river, but her tone brooked no disagreement.

"You know where you are leading. It's the worst kept secret in Honolulu. And it seems Lot is running out of time."

She'd been relieved to find Ani up and about when she and Malia returned from their ride with Kū in the vanguard. At least she wasn't on her death bed, which Ani seemed to believe the king was.

She swallowed and the bitter taste of bile reminded her of her earlier reaction. Hardly the response you'd wish for at mention of a future husband.

The worst thing was, Ani was right. She'd returned to Hawaii intent on protecting and expanding their family sugar business, and this partnership would enable her to realize that dream.

She'd known where they were heading, so why was she surprised? Max Moeller was regarded by everyone as a great catch. He enjoyed the respect of the king and the other members of the House of Nobles.

He would make an estimable father for any future children, something that until a few months ago hadn't concerned her. She'd always considered children something in her future, and she couldn't for the life of her work out why that had changed. The desire to have her own family had taken on much more importance in recent months.

Maybe that was because the three people—apart from Ani and Archie—she'd relied on as a child had all died suddenly, under shocking circumstances, earlier this year.

Or perhaps it was because she so wanted to banish from thought and mind the father who'd surfaced in her life during that grim time. Before July of this year, she'd always been told her father had died when she was a baby.

Now she knew the truth: that he was an avaricious big shot who'd tried to wreck the Manolo family sugar business because of a petty vendetta against her grandfather.

God protect her babies from men like Senator Hector de Vile. At least Max Moeller hit the mark on that score. He'd be a good father and an honorable husband. Wouldn't he?

Leilani reached out and scooped up a generous spoonful of purple taro poi from the carved calabash that sat in the middle of the table. She exchanged a quick charged look with Malia across the table. Her half-sister looked remarkably fresh and glowing after their early morning ride.

Lani dabbed her finger into poi paste on her plate and licked it, savoring the subtle candy flavor—rather like sweet potato—as she considered what to say next. She didn't want to provoke Ani's wrath any further. Before she'd assembled her thoughts into something coherent, Ani cleared her throat theatrically. It was an old habit she had for reclaiming the girls' attention.

"You can't spend your life having fun, Leilani. And I want to see you properly settled before I die. Lot feels the same way. You're our *kāhili*—our standard bearer—for the next generation."

Kāhili. The vibrant scarlet, yellow and orange-feathered pole banners which were always present when the king attended a formal gathering—a symbol of rightness and duty.

Ani was rolling on. "Goodness knows where this old kingdom is headed. But with people like you and Max there to help support the crown… Whoever is king—or queen—you can help hold things together."

Lani felt tears spring to her eyes and gritted her jaw to suppress them.

"Ani, don't talk like that, please. I can't stand it. You're going to be with us for a good time yet. You and Lot both."

"Now that's wishful thinking, girl, and we can't afford to indulge in that."

Ani's face was solemn, but her good eye still carried the fiery spark she and Malia knew so well. The old woman was like a torch that would not be doused until her last day.

Leilani stretched her arm out and squeezed her godmother's bony hand.

"Is the king really dying?"

"You know how it is, Leilani. He's been slowly declining for the last year or so, but his doctors are getting really worried. And this business about the water—it's getting him down. I suspect he'll rally once that's off his mind."

"And if I marry Max, Lot will immediately give his approval for the water? For us both? Our plantation will get rights in perpetuity regardless of what happens? I mean if either Max or I die, for example? It will be a pillar the family business can rely on?"

Ani considered her with a steely eye. "You take nothing for granted, do you, girl? If it's so important to get it down in writing, then call in that lawyer friend of Malia's. Have something drawn up for Lot's assent."

Leilani glanced from Ani's furrowed cheeks to Malia's glowing pink ones. "Would Titus do that for me?" She turned back to her venerable stepmother. "And would Lot agree?"

Ani's black eye bored into her. "You get it drawn up and I'll make sure he does. Before the end of the day."

Twelve

"Pali. Come here and see to my hair. It's so important I look good tonight."

Honey Cleveland studied herself in the mirror for the fifteenth time and picked up the horsehair brush from the dressing table. She was due at Washington Square for the Honolulu Christmas party of the year, and she couldn't afford to look anything but her best.

"Is this color flattering on me?"

She ran a light finger around the neckline of her low-cut lime-green evening gown. Her hand moved up to caress the sparkling emerald necklace that fell in tiers from her slender throat to her generous cleavage. Teardrop emerald earrings hung from her lobes. She'd pass muster nicely if Pali could dress her hair. Her hair—and her green-hazel eyes—looked good with the lime-green dress, but the buttery blonde locks massed around her face in an unruly tangle needed urgent attention.

"Now…" she gasped, as if she'd climbed several flights of steep stairs. "I need something done about this now." Her voice had a plaintive whine. She sounded like her small nephew when he demanded ice cream.

The Hawaiian woman hired by her mother via the good services of Samuel Pitcairn, the American consul in Honolulu, bustled to her side and stroked her long tresses.

Pali had dressed Queen Emma for several years, until the girl had fallen into an out-of-wedlock pregnancy that led to her dismissal. Most Hawaiians welcomed family expansion without question, but the queen was a staunch Anglican, and though not unkind, couldn't condone loose living. Regardless of Pali's lifestyle—and Honey didn't care what she did in her private life—she knew how to make a woman look good.

"Beautiful hair, Miss Cleveland. You have beautiful hair." The girl's soft voice was music to her ears. She moved to the dressing table with fluid grace.

As Honey gazed back at her reflection, she saw the rigid lines around her mouth relax. "Thank you, Pali. You're very kind. But we have to fix this…," she tugged at the hair at her right temple…, "so I'll look like I've spent all day out in the wind."

Pali giggled. "Hawaiian men, they like the windblown look."

Honey looked at her in the mirror, eyes wide with surprise.

It was the first glimpse she'd seen of Pali's true personality in the week they'd been together.

"I'm not looking to attract a Hawaiian man," she said, one eyebrow raised in a cheeky riposte. Pali cocked her head in a skeptical tilt.

Honey hesitated and clarified the statement. "A man who lives in Hawaii, yes. But not a Hawaiian man."

A look of understanding passed between them as they stared back at each other.

"And this is important to you, yes?" said Pali.

She was a slender young woman, Honey guessed she probably still hadn't seen her twentieth birthday, and her lithe form showed no evidence of forthcoming motherhood.

Suddenly she felt an irresistible urge to confide in another woman. Her mother refused to discuss anything she considered risqué—and pregnancy was definitely risqué—and there was no one here she could open up to.

"It is, yes, Pali," she said. "My family's future depends on it."

"And do you like him, this man from Hawaii who is not a Hawaiian?" Her deep brown eyes sparkled with mischief.

Honey pushed her hair back from her face, and studied herself in the mirror for a minute before answering.

"I like him all right. He's old and rich. He'll do." She raised her eyes to Pali's, still looking through the mirror. The girl had taken up the hairbrush and was sweeping her long butter-blonde tresses into order.

"It's something I have to do. For the family, you know?"

Her lips quirked up at the corners. "But I'll let you in on a secret. I don't like him as much as that Frenchman who's just arrived. I wouldn't mind getting my hands on him." Pali giggled.

Honey picked up the pot of scarlet lip cream and dabbed her lips with it. She made a pouting expression, bringing them together to even out the spread of the color.

She looked back at Pali, and the corners of her mouth drooped.

"Pity he won't do. He doesn't have enough money."

Thirteen

"So this is 'the real Hawaii.'"

Aristide gazed around him, marvelling at the double-storied white colonnaded home set in park-like grounds in the heart of Honolulu town. He could be standing before a mansion on San Francisco's ritzy Nob Hill.

Titus took two glasses of champagne from the loaded silver tray held by a servant at the ready in the entry. He swiveled on his heel and passed one straight on to Aristide.

"Not quite what your childhood picture books in France portrayed, I imagine. If you ever saw any pictures of Hawaii at all, they'd have been of women in grass skirts and coconut shell bras under swaying palms?" He grinned.

"Welcome to Honolulu society. We are talking of the social elite, of course, but I knew it would surprise you."

Titus had filled him in on the background as they'd strolled through dusty streets to the Christmas party at Washington Square, the home of the king's private secretary John Owen Dominis, his mother Mary, and Dominis's wife, the high-born Lydia Paki.

Guests in evening wear, the women a bright flock of hummingbirds in emerald and scarlet and turquoise, were pouring in, channeled by the double-columned classical porch that led to the front door. No street noise, no dust reached these palatial climes, just the aroma of barbecued pork and the ambrosial perfume from the majestic floral arrangement overflowing from a Grecian urn at the bottom of the stairs.

Beside it, a choir of sweet-faced children led by a baton-wielding choirmaster started up on *Hark the Herald Angels Sing*, their pure soprano voices swelling to fill the stairwell, the stairs patterned in striated rainbow colors from a stained-glass dome at the apex.

So this is Leilani's world.

The thought came, unbidden, but Aristide recognized it for what it was. An acknowledgment that he no more belonged in this rarified company than fleas belonged on the backs of the king's dogs.

A cavern of hopelessness opened up within him.

What am I thinking, turning up here unannounced, and dreaming something can come of it?

He took another small sip of champagne, swallowing defeat down with the fizz, and hugged the wall, observing the crowd without getting in anyone's way. But he wasn't giving up, not yet.

Then he heard Titus's voice above the children's singing.

"Aristide! Over here!" Titus was standing ten feet away, beckoning. Beside him stood Leilani Manolo and Max Moeller. The black hole within deepened.

As he dodged around guests to reach them, he kept his eyes fixed on Leilani. Tonight her cap-sleeved dress was of tangerine silk, the scooped neckline edged with cream lace, the skirt ruched down the front in diagonal bands, creating a rippling effect as it fell. Dark red lace emphasized the slender line of her waist, the slimness of her hips. The design finished at the hemline with a deeper red ruched band. The overall effect was simple, elegant, and glorious. At her side Max wore the military style gold-braided jacket that Aristide acknowledged with a pinch in his gut was a perfect match for the red dress.

He stretched out his hand to greet the plantation owner first. Max's hand was cold and dry, a sudden reminder that the man was long past his springtime. Aristide wondered if his heart was in the same antiquated state.

"Mr. Moeller. Nice to see you again."

Moeller fixed him with piercing obsidian eyes.

"You still here?" he barked.

Aristide laughed, though he felt no mirth.

"I am. Do you have an objection to that?"

It was the magnate's turn to fake mirth.

"No, of course not. I'm just not sure what could interest you, here in paradise."

Aristide lifted his eyes to speak to Leilani, but before he got a word out, new arrivals interrupted.

Malia and Honey appeared at Titus's side, accompanied by an elegantly suited older man who spoke first.

"Ah Moeller, there you are. The king's been asking when he'll see you next."

He hesitated and dipped his head in acknowledgment of the rest of the party.

"Forgive the rude interruption." He glanced around the group. "Leilani, Titus…" He trailed off when his eyes reached Aristide.

Titus stepped in. "We missed you at the consul's farewell the other night, David. Aristide, meet the king's chancellor, David Kinau. David. Meet Aristide Laurent, a French winemaker from San Francisco, here for a brief visit. Far too brief, I'd say."

Kinau shook hands. "Not investigating the opportunities for grape growing?"

Aristide smiled in denial.

"Not investigating grapes, sir. Although I understand there was a Spanish winemaker who produced a creditable red here years ago.

But no. Taking a break in our slow season."

"And are you enjoying what you see?"

"Very much, sir. Quite different from what I expected."

"Really? In what way?"

Aristide glanced to Leilani. They hadn't exchanged one word. She was studying him with quiet intensity.

He glanced back at David Kinau, and in the next instant Honey Cleveland edged forward.

"Mr. Laurent," she said with a delighted gush. "Delighted to see you."

"Miss Cleveland. I should have known a party girl like you wouldn't miss a night like tonight. Isn't it…," he flicked his eyes to Leilani, who was still watching him closely…, "remarkable. Remarkable hospitality, I mean. Quite something."

Honey squeezed past David Kinau and brazenly took Aristide's arm, glancing at Max Moeller, and then briefly at Leilani, as she did so.

"Any minute now Santa's arriving." Her voice rang with girlish excitement. "I'm so glad we haven't missed out."

She cast a calculating eye toward Leilani. "Aren't you glad, Miss Manolo?"

Leilani's face shadowed in confusion. "Glad? Ohhh… you mean about not missing out on Santa?"

She glanced up at Max, who was only fractionally taller than she was. "I guess there's a child hidden away in all of us, isn't there?"

Honey simpered in satisfaction.

"That's right. No matter what our age."

Max's cheeks dimpled as his jaw clenched.

She patted Aristide's arm in a proprietorial gesture.

"You can escort me in, Mr. Laurent. I wanted to talk to you, and I haven't had the chance so far. That's just not fair."

Aristide opened his mouth to reply and hesitated. An expectant hush had overtaken them. The choir had fallen silent. A loud bell started clanging, sounding like a schoolroom bell coming from outside.

The children cheered and rushed for the front door. The adults shrank even closer to the walls, Honey hanging determinedly on Aristide's arm in the squeeze to allow a corridor for the latest arrival, a jolly red-suited Santa Claus. He was swinging a large bronze hand bell overhead with his left arm, while he carried a rough sugar sack over his right shoulder.

As he stepped over the threshold, a matronly woman appeared at his side.

"Three cheers for Santa," she said in a commanding boom. Aristide guessed this was Mrs. Mary Dominis, the owner of Washington Square. a widow with the resilience of offshore kelp.

She'd survived and thrived despite the deaths of her two adolescent daughters at boarding school in America and her trader husband's disappearance on his way home from China with a shipload of furniture and finery for their half-built house.

For years she waited for him to return, pickled in grief that had turned her into a stone-willed matriarch who resented sharing her son with anyone, including his wife.

Just as Aristide was digesting her appearance, a man he took to be her son moved attentively to her side. In the clamor, Titus slipped beside him, sheltering Malia under one arm. He leaned in and whispered in his ear: "John Owen Dominis, the king's press secretary."

Dominis was a clipped, formal-looking fellow with a woolly black beard. There was something cold about him that chilled Aristide. He had no desire to meet him.

The children enthusiastically cheered Santa, and Mrs. Dominis led the stocky white-bearded figure to a pair of closed doors leading off the reception area. He hadn't noticed before, but the excited dancing children were now eagerly following.

Their hostess paused expectantly in front of the closed doors, and her son stepped forward and opened them with a flourish. Like the Pied Piper of Hamlin, Santa entered with a rollicking gait in his sloppy black gumboots, ringing his bell, ahead of a cloud of laughing, chattering children.

Through the doors stood a large Christmas tree, its fresh forest fragrance wafting on air warmed by dozens of burning candles that decorated its branches.

"Oh… look at that," said Honey, giving his arm another squeeze. "Isn't it beautiful?"

Aristide took in the sunshine color of her hair, the way her body-hugging lime-green gown and emerald necklace highlighted her hazel-green eyes. "Beautiful? Yes. I suppose it is."

Fourteen

Malia had disappeared with Titus into the music room, which opened from the parlor. Strains of a merry dance tune wafted through, and Leilani recognized her sister's buoyant touch on the keys. Malia's easy acceptance of Honolulu's most celebrated lawyer had blindsided her.

Titus had been a social fixture in town for a decade, but she hadn't known he and Malia were friends. She missed the security of having her sibling always at her side, her perceptive, comical commentary brightening the dullest occasion. She wondered uneasily what else she'd overlooked, preoccupied as she was with the sugar business.

Honey had inveigled her way into being Santa Claus's little helper, acting as his winsome assistant, handing out presents to excited children. And from what she could see, they had enlisted Aristide to detach gifts from the tree and hand them on to Honey and Santa Claus.

It was a badly kept secret that Max's bosom pal Ezra Chance— minister of the interior—was jolly St. Nick.

Even from her vantage point at the opposite side of the room, she could see Honey's satisfied glow. Aristide was enjoying himself too, smiling and chatting as he worked.

Around them, champagne glasses in hand, stood Honolulu's

younger set, egging them on, joking together. Alexander and Baldwin, the sugar factor men, and their young wives Polly and Dorothy. Theobald Goldsmith from Sun Insurance in London and his wife Cherry, Queen Emma's current fashion sage. Beside her, Henry Nolte, the tobacco merchant, and Mac McInerney, fabric importer and haberdasher… Honolulu's social up-and-comers were having a merry time.

Leilani's chest pinched.

Here she was, in contrast, stuck in the "old people's corner" with Max and David Kinau, engaged in a deep discussion about the King's wishes on some matter of household administration that held no interest for her.

In a nearby circle some of Honolulu's older socialites -the wives of the men who ran the town's businesses, newspapers and government - David Kinau's wife and mother amongst them - gossiped.

Her stomach clenched. Was this how life would be as Max's wife, if she accepted? Endless occasions glued to his side, a rich man's jewel, her input and opinions neither sought nor valued? Would she be able to continue to manage her own plantations? Once married, would Max ease her out of her role there too?

And when she had children—if not before—would she sidelined to hobnobbing with the older wives, stroking their vanities, sniffing out and sympathizing over domestic secrets that might forewarn Max of changes in their husbands' political or commercial interests?

She swallowed hard, the taste of ashes so real in her mouth she pulled back her shoulders with a sharp lift and gulped for air. She was suffocating, lost in a dispiriting reverie, and no one had even noticed. She felt relief, and then disappointment.

Would Aristide stand by like Max, oblivious to her thoughts and feelings, treating her like a piece of furniture? Or would he be flitting off after the next pretty young thing, just like he was now?

Max and David were rising, signaling they were retiring to the veranda for cigars. Max threw a shepherding arm lightly around the back of her waist, his attention perfectly proper, but subtly possessive.

He guided her out of the bright, cheerful room, the atmosphere fizzing with the joy of children and the promise of Christmas, out into the quiet night.

***

Leilani sat back in a woven bamboo basket chair and gazed up at the sliver of new moon suspended above her in a velvet sky. Was Archie up there somewhere, looking down on her? She smiled inside at the silliness of it, her fantastical thinking.

Her *hānai* grandfather—an adopted grandfather in the Hawaiian tradition—had died nearly a year ago now, and ever since he'd left them the family's sugar business had labored in turbulent seas.

Firstly Diamond had bought out the loyal export agency who'd been their reliable partner for years and declared the existing contract void. They offered them a tough new one, so cutthroat Leilani suspected it was designed to bankrupt them.

She'd gone to San Francisco, where she'd met Aristide, six months ago specifically to find another agent. Her mission was to guarantee the survival of Manolo Sugar, and she'd been successful in that.

She'd concluded bad blood from an ancient vendetta between Archie and the powerful US Senator, Hector de Vile, had been at the bottom of the problem. De Vile had a holding in Diamond, but she'd never found out what had gone wrong between them.

When she'd discovered, late in the piece, that de Vile was her father, it made it all so much worse. And she didn't care that de Vile had been kept in the dark as well. He'd had no idea she was his daughter.

She'd safeguarded the family's future with the agreement she'd made in San Francisco, but they still desperately needed to expand their production to thrive, and to do that they needed Kamehameha V's irrigation water.

She glanced across to the sofa where Max and David Kinau lounged. They were at ease, brandies at their elbows, heads haloed in pale blue cigar smoke, engaged in a low and intense discussion.

Max Moeller was a strikingly handsome man, she'd admit that. The allure of power clung to him like the smoke that wreathed his head, hard to resist. He acted like he was the answer to all her anxieties, and she'd wanted to believe he could be. After all, he had the ear of the king and his minister of the interior. What chance did she stand against that?

She enjoyed some status from her family, but increasingly it was the foreign—usually American—business and money men who held sway in the kingdom.

Rumor suggested Max controlled tonight's "Santa Claus"—Ezra Chance—because he'd lent him sizeable sums to cover the minister's gambling debts.

How was she going to go up against a power bloc like that? Was what Ani said true? If she refused this marriage, would she also forfeit access to water? Could she perhaps agree to a betrothal but bargain for a long settlement date?

She was toying with that idea when a big black moth fluttered across her line of sight. Moths of death, the villagers called them. They meant someone had died, or that someone dead was returning to say goodbye.

Ezra Chance glanced up and noticed the fluttering shadow. The candlelight picked up the light mauve bands that scalloped each wing, seeming to announce the creature as a sentinel of the soft violet night, a messenger from another realm.

"Lord have Mercy. Don't tell me our fears are about to be

realized." Grim shadows showed around Ezra's downturned mouth.

"What fears?" asked Leilani. "Max mentioned no fears to me."

"I wouldn't, would I?" A smile flickered across his lips.

"Why not?" Leilani asked. "I don't live a cosseted existence. I want to know what's happening in the world around me."

Her eyes sought Max's penetrating gaze.

"Archie always raised us to face life head on," she said. "I'm not planning to stop now he's no longer here."

Max shook his head fondly, as if humoring a child.

"There's no need, Leilani. No need for you to bother. I can take care of it."

"Take care of what?"

She could feel her body heat rising, the blood pulsing at her temples.

Ezra looked sheepish. "I think what Max is trying to protect you from, Leilani, is the possibility that Ani and Lot might pass on soon. Both of them. He wants that water business settled now, otherwise you might have to start all over again, negotiating with a new king. Or queen. If that happens, it could delay settlement by years. And in the meantime, it will hold your plantations as ransom."

Max was scowling at his friend, annoyed perhaps that he'd been so open with her.

"That will not happen, Leilani. Don't worry your pretty little head."

She turned toward the nightlight. The black moth had flown too close to the flame. It lay dying on the tabletop, scorched wings trembling. She bent over to pick up the fragile creature and cup it in her hands until it stilled.

Don't leave me, Archie. Tell me what I should do. I need you here now, more than ever.

Fifteen

"Come here, Aristide." Honey put out her hand to grasp his and gave him her most winning smile.

"Let's get a cool drink and go stroll in the gardens. It's a beautiful night out there. It's hot in here and I'm parched."

"Too much champagne, that's the problem. Try a glass of cool water instead."

"Water? What a spoilsport! And you a winemaker too… You should be ashamed of yourself."

She tilted her head at a coquettish angle and gazed into his eyes.

He stepped around her, out of her line of sight, and gently tapped her shoulders.

"It is hot in here. But I for one am drinking water only from now on."

He motioned to a server who quickly brought a tray loaded with champagne, fruit juice and water.

"I'm serious about the champagne," he said. "You'll have a cracking headache in the morning."

She tipped her head at a challenging angle and took another glass of champagne.

"No one has ever accused me of dying on a dunghill," she said.

Aristide's mouth twisted, and she laughed.

"What? You've never heard that before? I'm not one to give up without a fight. Now come on. There's something I want to show you."

They were exiting through the French doors onto the wide lanai that circled the house when Honey checked her forward movement. A woman was entering from the gardens.

"Why, Miss Manolo. Is it pleasant out?" She planted herself in Leilani's path, slowing her entry.

Leilani's eyes flicked from the blonde to Aristide, eyebrows momentarily hiked up in surprise. Her breathing quickened. "Very pleasant, Miss Cleveland. Thank you for asking."

Her deep chocolate eyes darted to Aristide's flushed face.

"Going for a stroll? It's beautiful out. The sky is purple and there's a new moon. Not sure if I'd call it a lover's moon, exactly. But you're the best judge of that, I'm sure."

She flashed a vague smile in Honey's direction, but her eyes did not reach to Honey's hazel-green peepers. Instead, she fixed her gaze on Honey's mouth and talked across a void to her white teeth.

"I was just going to look for Malia. I haven't seen her all night. I don't suppose you've any idea where she is?"

"Oh…" Honey's eyes flicked appreciatively to Aristide. "I think she and Titus are still in the music room. They're all having fun in there, playing and singing."

Leilani risked a quick flick to Honey's eyes. The younger woman's gaze focused on the dark space over Leilani's shoulder. "Max not with you?" She made a disapproving noise in her throat.

"That man really should learn to look after his women better."

She glanced down and twisted a large emerald ring on the middle finger of her right hand, as if reminding herself and everyone else that she was a woman of substance. The hint of a self-satisfied smile lurked at the corners of her mouth as she raised her gaze to Leilani's.

"We won't hold you up any longer…"

She reached out the be-ringed hand and hooked her fingers fast through Aristide's.

"The moon awaits…"

Sixteen

"That friend of yours is flying a bit close to the sun."

Leilani's coiled gut contracted into an even tighter ball. Her dress felt tight around her middle.

Max Moeller slumped back into an armchair in the music room. She corrected the observation. "Slumped," as far as a former military man allowed himself, which was only the slightest slouch of the shoulders for a lay person. He smiled across at her.

The Washington Square Christmas party was drawing to a close. Leilani tried to ignore the discomfort in her stomach.

The children had long ago gone to bed. The guests who remained sat around the warm room in intimate, quiet groups, replete with excellent food and an excess of wine, listening to the musicians who'd supplanted Titus and Malia's piano.

The air carried a drowsy scent of vanilla and beeswax candles, pierced with the fresh green upper notes from the newly milled Christmas tree.

A handsome, muscular Hawaiian plucked at a local guitar—copied and adapted from those introduced by Mexican vaqueros from California who'd brought longhorn cattle to Hawaii—a gift for King Kamehameha I in the 1820s.

With accompanying musicians also on guitars, they moved confidently from sea shanties to popular hymns, from local songs influenced by the mission hymns to an occasional Portuguese melody brought by plantation workers.

The night had reached that point where the remaining guests lounged with heavy-lidded eyes and leaden feet, and let the music soothe them, too weary to rouse themselves and go home.

Max Moeller took Leilani's hand, brought it up to his lips and brushed the briefest of kisses across it before lowering it again.

"Did I tell you how ravishing you look tonight?"

His straight white teeth shone in the soft lamplight. "Demure and desirable, all at once. Such a gift, Leilani. You truly are a remarkable woman."

She acknowledged the compliment with an appreciative smile.

"Thank you, Max. Very kind of you to say."

She glanced to where her hostess sat near the salon door, as if on guard for guests arriving or departing.

"Mrs. Dominis would have to be happy. She's done her guests proud. Pity Lot couldn't have been here. He'd have enjoyed it immensely."

"He would." Max paused, and Leilani sensed a stiffening in the fingers which still rested lightly on her arm.

"But as we've already mentioned, I'm afraid his days are in the counting."

Leilani's breath caught in her throat, and she made a little choking sound. "Aren't they for all of us, one way or another?"

She didn't want to think about Lot's death. Or Ani's.

She cast her gaze around her, noting the groups that clustered on settees, the younger ones settled on floor cushions.

No sign of Aristide. Or that Honey woman.

"What did you mean, a moment ago? When you said my friend

was flying too close to the sun?" She mastered her expression to show blank neutrality, as if the inquiry was of the merest passing interest. "What were you referring to?"

"Oh, come, Leilani. Playing the naïve ingenue doesn't become you." His tone was lightly mocking; one side of his mouth curled up in a question.

Her cheeks flushed hot despite her desperate attempt to play ignorant. She stayed silent until Max spoke again.

"Your San Francisco friend. The Frenchman. Honey Bancroft Cleveland has got a powerful father. If Gerald gets a whiff of scandal about her conduct here, Frenchie will be for the high jump. Cleveland will make sure he's unemployable in the Bay if he hears about it."

Max shot her a malicious smile, and the conviction that Gerald Cleveland *would* hear about it flooded through her.

"From what I saw tonight, she's being a naughty girl, and Gerald won't be pleased."

It took all her self-control to let her hands rest at her sides when she wanted to clutch at a stabbing pain in her chest.

"What you saw?" Leilani's voice had a telltale tremble.

"Let's just say that American gal can be reckless. She was leading the Frenchman down the garden path in more ways than one. If she got him into the glowworm grotto, I'd say he's a goner."

She willed herself to sound distant, disinterested.

"Max, really. It's nobody's business but theirs, surely. I understand he'd a talented winemaker, so it would be sad to see his career destroyed. But she doesn't strike me as a shrinking violet. And he's old enough to look after himself."

Seventeen

Honey led Aristide across the Iolani Palace lawn like a warrior queen who'd captured prize plunder. Exultation! Her veins sang with it. She clung to his hand.

Her fingers were stiff with intent, towing him after her, talking all the while and grateful that he was too much of a gentleman to object. She led with determined focus, certain of their destination, past garden bushes that released a full-bodied fruity aroma she could taste in her mouth.

She was twenty-three years old; she was a rich man's daughter, free of the usual constraints of her class, and she was having fun. She gave a throaty laugh and Aristide hauled back against her pulling arm.

"Slow down there, Honey. There's no emergency, is there?"

She turned to face him, still holding his hand, reluctant to let go.

"I'd like to be in on the joke. What's funny?"

Her eyes widened as she contemplated his chiseled face, half-obscured in moon shadow, long lashes casting a delicate fringe over the sharp line of his cheekbone. He was debonair and gentlemanly, and her father's spy was in no position to tell tales.

And if he did, she already had plenty of ammunition to silence him. Details he wouldn't be keen for either her father or the Hawaiian princess to know.

Aristide attempted to disengage from her, and she resisted.

"What's this all about?" Aristide's brows crinkled in a worried furrow that just made him all the more adorably vulnerable.

She allowed herself a long silence before she answered, enjoying her power.

"I told you. I have a surprise for you. Something I know you'll love to see." Her voice was level and husky, with no hint of indecision.

"Should we be doing this, Honey? Won't people talk?"

Honey fluttered her lashes.

"People talk? Of course they will talk. Why does that matter?"

"From what Titus says, your father is rather particular about who you see and what you do. Somehow I think haring off in the middle of the night with someone you've just met wouldn't qualify as appropriate."

She made a dismissive sound, blowing raspberries.

"How could he possibly object to a Christmas party at Washington Square with all the king's men?" She grinned. "You can't get much more respectable than that."

He pulled free of her hands and stepped away.

"What about Max Moeller?"

"What about him?"

"I got the impression at Titus's house the other day that you two were close. Won't he report back to your father?"

She put her hands on her hips and made a mocking dancer's bob.

"He won't be reporting anything back to my father. He might be a bit of a pompous grandad, but he's no fool."

She stepped in close and brushed one of Aristide's shoulders.

"How cute. That tree we passed has showered you in petals."

He stiffened and frowned at the familiar gesture.

"Honey…" A warning. His patience was unraveling.

She backed off, dropped the presumption.

"There's nothing serious going on between Max and me. We're

just having fun. But since you're asking, what about that Hawaiian princess from San Francisco? What's going on with you and her?"

The flicker on his jawline showed he'd gritted his teeth.

"Nothing."

His eyes were stormy.

"You've got no ideas there, have you?"

He turned away from her, and the dim moonlight highlighted spots of bright color on his cheekbone.

"Ideas? I hardly know Leilani, and it's clear her attention is otherwise engaged."

"I'm glad you can see that."

She glanced down at her feet, clad in lime-green satin slippers to match her dress. The dew on the lawn was seeping through the shiny fabric, and her feet were wet.

"Come on. My feet are getting cold. Let's see the glowworms."

She grabbed his hand again and turned and ran. This time he followed without objection.

She didn't slow until a dark pile of rocks loomed ahead. She dropped his hand and gestured.

"The Royal Spring. Very original name, isn't it?" She gave a low laugh. "But what it lacks in originality it makes up for in awesomeness."

***

Honey tiptoed ahead of him, through the dark cleft which signaled a cavern opening. The temperature was suddenly cooler, and Aristide heard the tinkling of water. The air had the clean smell of freshwater flowing out of the blackness.

The cavern opening was high and wide enough for two adults to enter side by side, although Honey still led the way and pulled him along behind her. They entered a high-walled cave which would easily hold ten people.

"Keep moving and watch your head." Honey glanced back at him, her eyes glittering.

The walls dripped, and in places green ferns sprang from their sides. A swampy odor, a mix of brackish water and green mustiness, enveloped them.

Honey drifted onwards through a narrower gap at the back of the cavern and around a sharp bend. They were now in pitch blackness, with no ambient light from outside, but within seconds the chilled air shimmered with a thousand sparkling spots of light, winking at them out of velvet inkiness.

Aristide's heart stilled. He had an impulse to reach out and touch.

"See?" Wonder echoed in Honey's whisper.

Her lips parted in a rapturous smile. The artifice of the worldly party girl had vanished. She radiated reverence as she gazed around her. Here was a woman Aristide could like.

"Wow!" he said. "This is amazing."

His work as a vintner meant dark cellars were like a second home, but the sudden beauty of the scene before him ambushed his senses. His skin tingled.

She turned to him.

"So you're glad I showed you?"

She was like a young girl seeking fatherly approval.

"I am. How did you know it was here?"

Her transparent joy dimmed.

"Max showed me," she said, mouth pouting.

"Max did?" He felt stupid repeating her words, but he was so surprised by the admission words failed him.

It wasn't something a man twice her age who was supposedly a guardian should do. Her change of mood was ample evidence something wasn't quite right.

"Why?"

She stared at him, her mouth set in a tight line.

"I mean. I know it's a lovely thing to see. But isn't it the wrong thing for him to be doing? He's supposed to be taking care of you on your father's behalf, isn't he? He's ardently wooing a woman not much older than you. It seems unusual on several counts."

He turned in a circle, taking in the scene again, licking his lips..

"Forgive me for commenting. But do you think it's OK? Really?"

She turned her back on him and stomped out. The winking lights instantly dimmed, as if their disagreement had disturbed the fireflies and they'd switched off.

He followed her out, the caress of the warm garden air warm on his cheeks after the cave's chill.

"Honey, stop. I'm sorry if I've offended you. I didn't mean to upset you."

She slowed her steps but continued walking.

"You're on the wrong track, Mr. Laurent. It's exactly what my father sent me here for. To win the heart of the pompous old goat."

Aristide felt a dry tickle at the back of his throat.

"He did?" His voice was raspy and uncertain. "Why on earth would he want you to do that?"

"Because Father's gambled away our money. Mother would turn in her grave if she knew. Half of it came from her family. Max bailed him out of debt. If I can entice him into the family, then 'Taa raa…'" She made a flamboyant gesture like a circus master announcing the next big act. "The debt will be forgiven and the Cleveland family can start spending again."

She stared at him determinedly.

"Why do you think I'm here in Hawaii? It's hardly San Fran, the 'Paris of the West,' is it? My father's hoping I'll pull off a rescue of the family fortunes."

"So… kind of like an arranged marriage?" said Aristide.

She gave a dull laugh. "Kind of… Except Max never misses an opportunity to advance his personal interests. He sees more advantage in marrying Princess Hawaii than he does a Cleveland heiress to nothing-much-at-all."

"Advantage? How?"

"He already controls a major share in our company, now he's got most of Father's share. He can pull the plug on us any time he chooses. He's realized by teaming up with Leilani he can get access to water to expand production—making himself a lot richer."

Honey spotted a garden bench and wandered over and sat down. Aristide remained where he was, regarding her.

Has she guessed I'm in love with Leilani? Maybe she's hoping I'll come between Lani and Max. Then the field will be open for her to move in and claim the prize.

He perched on the end of the bench, out of reach. Honey was lost in her own story.

"He's quite blatant about it. He sees the King has a soft spot for Miss Manolo, so he's sticking with her and going along for the ride."

Aristide's heart contracted.

Is she telling me this to get my hopes up? She's no fool, this blonde party girl, even though she likes to play at being one. Can I trust a word she's saying?

He readjusted his weight on the seat.

"So you're saying he's not genuine? He's only interested in the money?'

"Max is always only interested in the money. Nothing else counts."

Aristide perched on the wooden edge, reassured by the hardness digging into his buttocks. At this moment, the king's solid garden seat felt like the only thing in his world he could count on.

Eighteen

It was ridiculously early to be calling uninvited on Honey Cleveland, and Leilani knew it. But Max's unconcealed delight at the prospect of dirtying Aristide's reputation with Gerald Cleveland had disturbed her more than she wanted to admit.

She'd tossed and turned all night, feeling somehow responsible. If he hadn't made this wildly misguided visit to Hawaii to see her—and she was certain that was what motivated him—he'd never have got tangled in Honey's predatory claws.

As soon as Honey's housekeeper let her in and disappeared to somewhere else in the house, she plunged on with the speech she'd been rehearsing to herself all night.

"I wanted to warn you. Max is reporting back to your father. You need to be more careful."

Honey Cleveland threw back her head and let rip with a full-throated howl, putting her hand up to her mouth and gasping for breath between gales of laughter. When she regained her composure, she waggled her finger at Leilani, like a reproving governess.

"I need to be more careful? Why do you think I made a play for your French friend? I wanted to be noticed. I like being notorious. What would be the point otherwise?"

Leilani glanced uncertainly around the lavish drawing room, decked out in a blend of relaxed Hawaiian comfort and American good taste. Whoever had chosen the furnishings had an exquisite eye for design and a generous budget.

Gerald Cleveland had long maintained a home a street away from the palace, but Leilani had never visited before. She glanced at the seductive blonde lounging on the sofa before her, her arms extended along the wide back, positioned to lay claim to the entire room.

"I don't understand. Why would you want to be notorious?"

Honey Bancroft Cleveland's eyes twinkled and her pretty rosebud mouth pouted.

"Well, that's a personal matter that I'm not at liberty to discuss with Max's wife-to-be. But thank you for coming all the way from the palace to warn me of the obvious." She broke into another tinkling laugh, and although there wasn't a hint of malice in it, Leilani felt her cheeks flush red.

Then the embarrassment instantly turned to anger.

"You might not suffer, Miss Cleveland, because no doubt you're Daddy's little angel. But spare a thought for someone like Aristide. He's an immigrant winemaker with no particular clout.

"And I'm concerned Max is going to make things difficult for him with your father. If he loses his job…"

Honey clapped her hands. Her eyes sparkled with mischief. "Ohhh… That's why you're here… You're worried about Aristide."

Her green-flecked eyes were soft and amused.

"I'm so glad you came. Do sit down and I'll order up coffee. This is going to take a little time to explain."

The housekeeper brought the coffee, and Honey launched into her story.

"Don't worry, Leilani. It's not what you think. Max has got my father over a barrel, because of gambling debts and the IOUs. Max basically owns our family. And my father is powerless to do anything about it, although of course the public doesn't have a clue the Cleveland name is worthless. It suits Max and Father to leave it that way."

Leilani gaped. In spite of herself, she liked, even admired, this feisty young woman, fighting to clean up her indulgent father's mess.

She fought back a rising nausea as she thought of the months when she'd battled to find a sugar agent after Diamond took over. She'd blamed her father, Hector de Vile, for the problems they'd faced.

"Max? Max is the power behind Diamond Sugar? Are you certain?"

She knew her voice had a desperate, disbelieving edge. This man who'd painted a picture of them working together to create a great joint sugar company, had been orchestrating her destruction for the last year? The only thing that saved them was the young manager at Pike Consulting, Will Davenport, and his willingness to act as their importer.

"Quite sure," said Honey. "He sees it as part of his arsenal. 'All's fair in love and war' and all that. It's his motto in life. I know he's intent on marrying you—on the one hand. And he's determined his business will come out on top—on the other. He doesn't believe in 'equal players.' Just winners and losers."

She grinned. "He probably considers you're a winner if you nab him."

Leilani shuddered. "I can't believe the deviousness, the duplicity of the man. And to think I blamed Senator de Vile…"

She turned her coffee cup in her saucer, fiddling idly as she considered all that Honey had spilled over this highly informative coffee session. She shook her head as a crazy mirth bubbled up from inside her. She gasped from trying to hold it down.

"I came here thinking I was doing you a favor… and my

goodness… I had no idea… I knew nothing. I'm so sorry to have been so presumptuous. I really am. I didn't give you credit for having a brain."

"Don't worry. That's a mistake a lot of people make." Honey laughed with her. "I don't mind. I can use it to my advantage."

"Oh? Like when?" Leilani was intrigued.

"Like when I'm dangling Aristide in front of Max." She gave Leilani a wicked grin. "Seems as if it's working, if he's threatening to tittle-tattle to Father."

Leilani felt a pang of concern for the young woman opposite her, let down by those around her as badly as Leilani herself had been.

"What's your end game, Honey? Why are you here, in Honolulu? And what do you hope to get out of it?"

There was a loud rap at the door and Honey's housekeeper rushed in.

"Miss Cleveland… Your visitor… There's someone here for her, and he says it's urgent."

Max's bulk loomed in the doorway behind her. He glowered at Leilani from the doorway.

"It would be convenient if you let me know where you're going. Even your sister didn't have a clue. And this is the last place I would have expected to find you."

"Really, Max? And why is that?"

Honey rose with a coquettish air and crossed the room to greet him, her playgirl face firmly in place.

"Aren't we allowed to get together for a girlie chat? Just because we're not doing needlepoint…"

She trilled with laughter and turned back to Leilani.

She stood, her arms crossed, staring at them with a worried frown.

"Why are you here, Max? What's happened?"

"It's Ani. You're needed immediately. She's asking for you."

Nineteen

"Ani."

Leilani slowed her run at Ani's doorway. She smoothed her skirt and pushed her hair back off her face before pushing through fringed Chinese silk drapery that formed a diaphanous veil between Ani and the rest of the domestic to-ing and fro-ing.

Leilani suspected her *hānai* Mum preferred the silk curtain to a sturdy door because it made it easier for her to eavesdrop on everything going on around her.

But now as she lay back on her pillows, her eyes fluttered like a moth around a light, unfocused on anything except the nearest and most obvious object.

Her steely penetration, the resolute will which was her hallmark, seemed to have left the frail, wizened form that gazed up at her from dazzling white pillows embroidered with the royal insignia.

Leilani had rushed here, ignoring Max's calls to slow down, wanting nothing else but to get to Ani. And as she gazed at the woman who'd been the closest thing she'd had to a mother for as long as she could remember, she saw Ani was not staging a royal command performance to get her own way.

Her eyes were dull and rheumy. She rolled her head from side to side, unable to settle. Her skeletal hands clutched at the top sheet, and as Leilani stood at her bedside, she gave a sudden sharp cry.

"Ani! Are you in pain?" Ani's matronly attendant Luana appeared at the other side of the bed, holding out a glass of water and some pills.

"Has she taken any pain killers?"

Luana nodded. "Yes, she has, but perhaps she needs more."

Ani glared at Luana, suddenly focused.

"No," she croaked. "Not now. I need a clear head to talk to Leilani."

Leilani perched tentatively on the edge of Ani's big flat bed and stroked her hair. "We don't need to talk now. We can do that later…"

"No. No we can't. We have to talk now. Tell me what's been going on. Where have you been? I heard you go out this morning."

So Leilani told her. About Max controlling Diamond Sugar. About his pursuit of Honey Cleveland at the same time as he was declaring his interest in her. In a quiet, controlled voice she let it all spill out. As she talked, Ani's fretfulness eased. She stopped rolling about on her pillows, and her clear eye hardened into a dark pinpoint of concentration.

When Leilani fell silent, there was a long, pregnant pause.

"What you're telling me, Leilani, it's not surprising, is it? It's normal for men like Max, who are used to getting their own way. Those sorts of men only play by their own rules. That's how they've gotten where they are. Surely you see that?"

Leilani's gut felt loaded with rocks, but she nodded her silent assent.

"The thing is, when you are on his side, then you win too. He looks after you like he looks after himself. That's why we need this marriage to go ahead."

She reached out her bony right hand and gripped Leilani's forearm with surprising strength.

"I'm dying, Leilani. I want to see our family heritage secured before I go."

"So you think I shouldn't care that Max tried to bankrupt us? To lock us out of exporting? All's fair in love and war, like Honey said? Is that it?"

Leilani could feel the hot lava flow of anger rising within her, though she tried to keep her voice light.

But Ani wasn't listening.

Her fingers slackened on Leilani's hand and her eyes drooped shut. Within seconds, she was asleep.

***

It was early afternoon before Ani woke, refreshed and hungry. Luana brought her a lunch of fish laulau—tuna wrapped in taro leaves and slow cooked until the taro tasted like spinach. Dr. George visited but when Leilani tried to question him discreetly outside Ani's room, he refused to give an opinion on whether the setback was temporary or something more serious.

"Her heart is very weak, Leilani. The best we can do is ensure she gets full rest and see what happens." Dr. George left promising to call again first thing in the morning.

Leilani and Malia brought comfortable armchairs into Ani's room and settled in to keep watch, one on each side of her bed, but it soon became clear Ani was feeling much better and was impatient to get up.

"You're not doing that until Dr. George has been tomorrow—at the very earliest—so just lie back and enjoy a rest. Goodness knows you deserve it."

She stroked the top of Ani's head, smoothing strands that had escaped from her hair out of her eyes.

"You remember I was telling you about going to see Honey

Cleveland this morning, before we came to see you? And I think your attitude was I shouldn't let that bother me…?" She paused. Ani raised her eyebrows but remain silent.

"I'd assumed it was Hector de Vile who caused trouble for us with Diamond. It turns out it probably wasn't de Vile, it was Max—but de Vile would be the same sort of man, wouldn't he? They'd be pretty alike? They're much the same age for a start. So if you think Max is OK, why didn't you approve of Hector de Vile? Because I suspect you don't approve of him. Is that right?"

Ani linked her fingers together over the top of her sheet and moistened her lips with her tongue. She turned to Malia and gestured to the glass on the bedside table.

"Get me some water, would you Malia, dear? I can't answer your sister's questions when I'm so dry."

Malia returned in a few minutes with a pitcher of water and poured a glass for her. Propped up on her pillows, Ani sipped contentedly.

"You're right, Leilani. I didn't approve of him. I think that was because he encouraged your mother's wild side. And he had no respect for the old customs. She had status in the kingdom. He was a nobody."

"Is that why Archie objected too? I mean, if he really was our father, why didn't they get married? I thought that's something Archie would have wanted."

She didn't know why it had taken her so long to ask the question. When she'd first got home from San Francisco weeks ago, she'd wanted to put everything that had happened in California behind her. To block all acknowledgment of her newly discovered father.

She'd adamantly refused to meet with him, even though he'd made it plain he wanted to talk. She couldn't forgive that he'd opposed their business interests at every turn. That's what she'd thought he'd done, anyway. And he'd encouraged Cyrus in a ridiculous "friendly abduction" at one point.

If I pretend he's not my father, then he isn't, her heart whispered.

She'd allowed that whisper to harden into conviction. But that had changed this morning, with the revelation that it was Max rather de Vile who'd been intent on ruining them. She couldn't avoid facing up to her questions any longer. Much as she hated the idea, she had to learn everything she could about Hector de Vile and the rift that that developed into a full-blown feud between him and her grandfather.

It must have been over her mother, surely. So what happened all those years ago?

Ani flicked her index finger against the rim of the empty crystal glass she still nursed in her hands, making a clear, bell-like note which brought Leilani's attention back to the calm room, and her *hānai* mother's drawn, gray face.

Ani was gazing at her with a faraway stare, intent on some long past scene rather than the palace sickroom. She licked her lips and when she spoke her voice was rasping and dry, like chalk on a blackboard.

"They did get married. What makes you think they didn't?"

Twenty

They did get married.

Ani's voice had been cool, pragmatic, carrying no ring of approval or condemnation.

What makes me think they didn't?

Leilani's lungs felt short of air. Her breath came in rapid, shallow puffs. She could feel hot anger rising inside.

"I suppose because there's been no suggestion they divorced. And Hector isn't Malia's father. Matthew Lilolilo is. What happened? I don't understand."

She glanced at Malia, who sat as still as Kapaliokamoa, Oahu's oddly shaped ancient lava pillar the old people called the cliff of the chicken.

"And how come no one's told Kaleo and me about it?"

Ani shrugged irritably, as if already bored.

"A million reasons. Starting with you didn't ask, it doesn't matter, and why would anyone care…? Really, Leilani. Its ancient history. You weren't born when they went their separate ways. Your mother married Matthew Lilolilo. He was always your 'real father.'"

Leilani's inner compass swung wildly. Her eyes shot to Malia, who gave her the tiniest nod. She too had noticed Ani's subtle change of mood. The older woman's expression softened, her voice turned liquid, as she spoke the name of the man she and her brother always believed was their father. Matthew Lilolilo Manolo.

They bore his surname, although the sugar plantations came from her mother's and grandfather's estates. Matthew died in a shark attack a few months after their first birthday, and Archie and others, like Bully Pike and Cyrus May, stood in as father figures for the rest of their childhood.

Leilani framed her response carefully, judging Ani might not be as reluctant to discuss Lilolilo as the rest of it.

"Lilolilo. Did you know him too?"

Her wizened face took on a moony tenderness.

"We grew up together. He was such a handsome man."

"And was he good to our mother?" Malia hadn't spoken, but now she interjected. Leilani watched the ropey tendon knot in Ani's neck.

"He tried his best. Your mother was hard to please."

"In what way?"

Ani shrugged. "She just was."

"And what happened to de Vile then? Why did he leave her? Leave us?" This was Leilani's quest. Malia couldn't care less about de Vile. He wasn't her father, she'd never met the man, and she had no interest in doing so. Leilani, on the other hand, couldn't get him out of her mind.

"If you must know, Leilani, he didn't have any choice. De Vile and Abigail married without Archie's permission, village style, not in a church. Your mother was already pregnant. Archie was livid."

Her mouth took on a grim twist.

"He'd raised her from birth, he and Connie. They were her *hānai* parents. The king of that time gave her to them because the Arnolds were childless. In Hawaiian society that was frowned upon

"Then after all their efforts to raise her a good young Christian lady, she goes wild with a sea captain and marries him without her father's consent. Archie couldn't have that, so while de Vile was away at sea, he had the marriage dissolved according to our customs, and he married her off to Lilolilo instead. In the church this time. When Hector came home from sea, he discovered they had given his wife to someone else. Just like in the Bible, when King Saul gave David's wife Michal away. Just like that.""

Leilani's heart turned over in her chest. Much as she loathed de Vile, he'd endured public humiliation. And if he'd had feelings for their mother, who they'd been told was the "beauty of her generation," it must also have been privately crushing.

"Did he mind? Lilolilo, I mean." Malia was interested in Matthew, naturally. She was like Kāne and Kū, nose to the ground, hot on the scent of discovery. Leilani felt her insides quaking with silent laughter at her sister's sudden interest.

Ani sat silent as stone for a long time, contemplating her linked hands in her lap. She gave a long, painful sigh.

"Matthew and I… we were planning to marry… we were getting ready to ask his father's permission… but that wasn't to be. Obviously. Abigail came first."

She spat the words with a bitter edge. She sighed and added as an afterthought, "Lilolilo? He did his best."

Leilani thought how strange life was. This woman had raised the children of her bitter rival, and they hadn't even realized it.

"Ani, I'm sorry to keep coming back to de Vile. I can tell you don't want to talk about him. You probably didn't like him."

She paused, as if to allow time for Ani to comment, but the old woman's lips set in a hard line.

"I've got to ask. Is that why de Vile hated our grandfather? Because he took away our mother? Or was there something else? He took the message on board, didn't he? He never came near us, ever again. Not once. Ever."

Under her dull pallor, Leilani could see the question disturbed Ani. Her face turned a disagreeable pale purple.

"Leilani, why are you wasting your energy on all this old stuff? It's up to you girls to make sure something of your lives. It's too late for me and mine to make a difference. That's why I keep telling you. Time is short. Lot and I won't be here for much longer. And we want things settled before we go."

Leilani's jaw tightened at Ani's sudden change of temper. She caught Malia's raised eyebrows, which had shot up under her long fringe.

For a few seconds, she thought of Matthew Manolo, coerced into marrying her mother "for the good of the family and nation."

Was that what Ani was doing to her? Punishing her because she'd missed out on her man, and she saw no reason why Leilani shouldn't pay the same price?

I couldn't have the man I wanted, so why should you?

And wasn't Ani right? She'd told Aristide she had to come back to Hawaii to make sure the family fortunes were on a sound foundation. She'd committed to care for Malia and future generations, and she still had the chance to keep that promise.

So why did she get this rocks-in-her-stomach feeling whenever she contemplated being Max's wife?

Her eyes flicked to Malia, who was watching her intently, the faintest hint of a knowing smile on her lips. What was she so smug about?

"You're right, Ani. We have responsibilities others might not carry, don't we? It's naïve of me to think a man of Max's experience would restrict himself to one woman."

Her gaze ping-ponged between Malia and Ani, though she avoided looking directly at either of them.

"I don't know what I was thinking. I'm still furious about the way he's conducted this sugar business, but I'll get over it. You're right. When we're married, his interests and mine will coincide, so we shouldn't have anything to worry about."

She glanced across Ani's bed linen to Malia.

"I guess we'd better hurry up that dressmaker to put the finishing touches to our wedding garb—your bridesmaid dress and my bride one. We've only got a couple of days."

She smiled at Ani.

This is what counts. Giving Ani peace in her old age. She sacrificed so much for us.

Ani settled her bony shoulders back into the pillows.

"Now you're talking sense. I knew you'd see where your duty lies."

Leilani acknowledged a fleeting wish, like a scudding gray cloud in a pale sky. A wish that doing your duty didn't feel like locking a steel band across your chest.

She shook her head, pushing the vagrant thought away.

I can do this. It's why I came home, isn't it? To secure my family's future.

Twenty-one

"Honey. What are you doing here?"

Leilani had just left dressmaker Rose Penny's salon, where she'd had the last fitting for the wedding dress she would wear in two days' time. As she'd stepped onto Merchant Street's brick sidewalk she'd spotted Honey, lingering in front of the fashion store, twirling a parasol that matched her turquoise dress. Leilani got the distinct impression she was waiting for her.

"Why, I thought it would be nice to have a girls' catch-up. We didn't finish our chat from a few days ago because of your family emergency."

Honey gave her a conspiratorial smile. "In another couple of days you'll be Mrs. Max Moeller and far too taken up with your marital duties to have time for girlfriends, I'm sure."

Leilani glanced from her smiling mouth to her eyes, which were sharp and unamused.

"A girlfriend chat. Of course. Where do you propose to have this little tête-à-tête?"

"My house is just round the corner. Why not come home with me and have iced tea on the lanai."

Leilani had made planning for her coming nuptials the focus of all her attention—that and making sure Ani was being well looked after. She told herself this was her destiny—to secure her family's future, even if it was at some personal cost. In a grown-up world you couldn't expect things to have a fairy-tale ending, could you?

Max seemed to have reformed his behavior since the night of the Christmas party, when he'd alternately ignored her in favor of talking business with David Kinau or subtly baited her about Aristide.

He'd been attentive and considerate to both her and Ani, arranging delivery of the fresh tuna, taro and pineapple he knew the old lady loved, continuing to reassure her that things were moving to a satisfactory conclusion with the vexed issue of the plantation water supply.

"Lot will sign the water lease just as soon as we're married," he assured her.

As they strolled toward Honey's King Street home, the American kept up good-natured chatter on the latest gossip from the Ladies Circle—which merchants had the best European fabrics in their warehouses from San Francisco and Bremen. Why the whaling fleet that had just left port at the end of the season wasn't likely to return in anything like the same numbers next year. And the delightful scandal surrounding the Royal Hawaiian Theatre show with tragedienne Rose Evans. *Lady Audley's Secret* was delighting full houses.

"It's a sensational story of accidental bigamy, did you know?" Honey paused on her front-door steps and turned to Leilani with a glint of glee in her green-flecked eyes.

"And of a woman determined to follow her own wishes, regardless."

Leilani stared at her.

"Why do I get the feeling there's nothing about this little get-together that is spontaneous? What's the idea, Honey? Are you trying to tell me something?"

Honey turned with a swish of her rose petal skirts and entered the wide hallway.

"I'm not trying to tell you anything, but I have someone here who is…"

The Cleveland drawing room seemed dark after the dazzling sunlight outside, but it took Leilani only seconds to recognize the figure who rose as they entered. Aristide Laurent. Even silhouetted against the light from the windows, she'd know him anywhere. Her heart stuttered in her chest. She glanced at Honey, and then back to Aristide.

"What… what's going on? What are you two playing at?"

She sounded upset. Almost fearful.

"I need to speak to you, Leilani. It's important, and it didn't seem appropriate to come begging to the palace. I thought Max's lackeys might throw me out." Aristide took a step toward her and then stopped himself.

Honey cut in.

"I offered to act as the intermediary. But now I've got you together, I'm leaving you to it."

She and Aristide exchanged understanding looks.

"Good luck. I suspect you're going to need it."

The door closed behind her, leaving Leilani gaping at Aristide across an awkward silence.

"I don't believe this. You appreciate it's highly improper, to set me up like this. I am marrying a privy councillor the day after tomorrow. You do get it? Such men don't take kindly to their betrothed slipping off to secret assignations."

The angry determination in her voice contradicted the anxious flutter in her belly. She was churning with uncertainty. Aristide Laurent was in her past. Max was her future. It terrified her to look back in case she preferred the memory of what had been to the hope of what was to come.

"That's what I want to talk about, Leilani."

He gazed at her with appeal in his eyes.

"Sit down, Lani. Please. Give me a few minutes to explain."

"There is no need for me to sit down. I'm not staying. Say what you have to say and I'll go."

His eyes narrowed and the skin across his cheekbones tightened.

"Very well, then. As you want it."

He closed the gap between them by another step and then hesitated.

"Leilani, there's something I haven't told you. I haven't kept it deliberately from you. It's just we haven't had a proper talk since I arrived."

Her forehead creased in confusion.

"I have no idea what you're talking about. You must make it clearer than this."

"Very well. I've got information about Max that you should know. I'm reluctant because you'll obviously consider me an unreliable witness where he's concerned. But I can't stand by and do nothing."

"Information? From where? I wasn't aware you moved in the same circles as Max. Here or in San Francisco."

An ice-cold pause lengthened between them. Leilani shivered. Although the sun was still bright outside the windows, in this room she felt as if the temperature had dropped by twenty degrees.

"From someone who moves in the same circles." He hesitated again, reluctant to continue.

"Go on," she said impatiently. "I haven't got all day. Who gave you this 'information'?"

Another long pause, and then he took a deep breath.

"Your father."

She saw black spots dancing before her eyes. She clenched her fists.

"You've been speaking with my father?" The incredulity in her voice rang in the room.

"Yes."

"I don't believe it. How could you?" She could hear the hurt too. Didn't he understand he was trading with the enemy? "When?"

"Before I came here."

"And what has he got to say about anything to do with my life? For goodness' sake, Aristide, you know how I feel about him…"

"Leilani, he's not as bad as you think. He really wants to talk to you, to explain his side of things. And he's known Max a very long time."

She didn't want to hear any more.

She whirled on her heels to make for the door and then turned back angrily.

"I can't believe this. You know how badly he betrayed me. You better than anyone know I can't stand to hear his name. Has Honey cooked up that story about Max owning a controlling interest in Diamond Sugar as part of this charade? What is this? A plot to break Max and I up so Honey can swoop in and save the family business? Do you think I'm stupid?"

He reached out to take her arm, to placate her, and then thought better of it. He stepped away instead.

"I know very well you're not stupid, Leilani. And I don't have documentary evidence. It's still coming. But I have to tell you. Hector says Max is married. He's got a wife in Hungary. If she's still alive, he's about to commit bigamy."

A blinding red wave swelled before her eyes. Her ears thrummed with the roar of blood rushing to her head.

"Hector says?" The words exploded out of her mouth like vomit, bitter and mocking and unstoppable. "And the evidence is still coming?"

She sneered.

"How is it that not a soul on earth except Senator Hector de Vile knows anything about it? Hector, who until a few weeks ago, acted like my sworn enemy. Like our sworn enemy. He tried to destroy you too. I can't believe you've cozied up to him and fallen for his poisonous nonsense."

She took two more steps to the door and then whirled back to him.

"Besides, if it was true, the king would know. And staunch Anglican that he is, he wouldn't allow it."

She bit her lip, as if trying to press back her angry rant, but with the next breath it was clear she'd failed.

"Really, Aristide, I didn't think you'd be so pathetic. You're a sore loser, and you're wasting my time.

"I've got a darling *Mère* who needs nursing back to life. I've got a man to marry and a business to run. And you coming peddling this malicious gossip is … It's horrible."

She shuddered. "I thought you were a better man than this, Aristide. I really did."

She turned and fled.

Twenty-two

Leilani could have walked to the altar, across the Iolani Palace grounds, but she arrived in a greenery-festooned carriage, alighting to the cheers of well-wishers gathered around the Pro Cathedral's arched entryway. These were the folk who'd arrived too late, or weren't important enough to claim a seat in the already overflowing pews inside.

She descended from the carriage in the cream silk gown she'd convinced Ani was all she needed, and the growling nausea she'd experienced ever since she'd woken melted as she smiled and gestured to the townspeople she recognized—the beach boys and plantation workers, nursemaids and shop workers, the fishermen and their wives who were there to ogle at her dress and wish her well.

The sight of them lifted her flagging spirits, and she felt a surge of hope.

It's going to work out all right, isn't it? I've just got a severe case of nerves.

She took the arm of the man King Lot had designated to "give her away"—his majesty's minister and last week's Santa Claus, Ezra Chance—and allowed him to lead her into the small wooden church, no grander than the simplest village chapel, built on land gifted from the royal gardens by the previous king and his wife Queen Emma. The dowager queen was heading a vigorous campaign to build a much grander limestone cathedral modeled on French Gothic lines, but that was still on the drawing board.

Inside, light cascaded through the arched chapel windows, and her heart lifted further. It reminded her of the Biblical storybooks Archie had read her as a child, where just this kind of slanting light accompanied miracles. She'd always thought of it as "light from Heaven."

Well, maybe this isn't from Heaven, exactly, but it reminds me miracles can happen.

She lifted her eyes to search out her groom. Max stood in the nave's head, an imposing, broad-shouldered figure in his military jacket with the gold epaulets. His stance said it all. Handsome. Resolute. A man you could rely on. This was it. She was looking at the father of her future children, the bulwark who'd be at her side when they negotiated the storms and losses she knew were coming.

The solemn chords of *Here Comes the Bride* rang out, vibrating through the wooden floor as they neared the organ loft. Leilani could smell the fragrance of the posies tied to the end of each pew, the mixture of lemony, minty, and fresh green aromas from the native flowers and herbs reminding her she was in her Honolulu home, walking into an important new phase of life.

Her eyes flicked to the left side of the nave, where Malia and Titus, Ani and all the other Manolo cousins and connections sat. She spotted Ani in the front row, eye-catching in an amethyst taffeta gown with a ruffled neckline and a gorgeous brightly colored feathered cape that wrapped around her shoulders. Her cheeks were pinker, her complexion more vital than it had been in weeks. She looked every bit as composed and regal as the dowager queen who sat next to her.

Leilani allowed a very slight smile to play across her lips. This day was as much for Ani as it was for her. No matter what happened now, Ani could retire from her family duties, satisfied she'd handed stewardship over to Max.

From Ani she searched out Malia, further along the pew, looking incandescent in a light apricot gown with a matching muslin wrap and coral earrings that set off her elegant swan-like neck to great advantage, leaning ever so slightly into Titus's gray-suited shoulder. She gave another quick smile. Betrayed by their body language.

What a fine pair they made. Her eyes moved involuntarily down the row, though she didn't want them to. No sign of Aristide. Her stomach lurched as he came to mind. Since their last conversation, she couldn't even think of him without flushing with volcanic anger tinged with deep disappointment.

If only he'd understood that she had to do this. It was what her family and country required. It was best that he stay away. He might even be readying to leave Honolulu, and that was a good thing.

She arrived at Max's side and he cast his eyes toward her without fully turning his body to face hers. His deep brown irises shone with approval. He leaned forward and whispered in her ear. "You look exquisite, Leilani. I'm proud to have you as my wife."

Her heart turned warm and liquid.

Yes. This is going to be all right. More than all right.

Honolulu's Anglican Bishop Thomas Nettleship Staley came forward to greet them. He'd been in the kingdom for eight years and shared the sorrows and joys in the royal household. He now reached out his hands and took one of Leilani's in both of his. He'd arrived on the island only a few weeks after the death of the previous king's only son, and he'd also conducted that king's funeral barely a year later.

He'd happily agreed to the present king's request to grant them a common license so they could wed without the customary banns being read over the preceding three weeks.

"We want this wedding to happen while her mother is still here to bless her," the king had explained. Now the bishop leaned forward, his face shining with refined approval.

"Welcome, my dear Leilani, on this auspicious occasion. Max, I am sure, today you're a proud man."

The bishop had deep-set dark eyes under black brows and a kind, finely shaped mouth.

"Shall we get started?" he asked softly, as he lifted his eyes to the expectant congregation and opened with a greeting and first prayer.

"We are gathered here today to join Leilani Lilolilo Manolo and Maximillian Jonas Moeller in holy matrimony."

Leilani glanced up into Max's face and over his shoulder. Light flickered from a tall brass candelabra behind him, and she gazed at the sparkling light, momentarily dazed.

"Send your Holy Spirit

And pour into our hearts

That most excellent gift of love,

That we may worship you now..."

The bishop's commanding bass, his familiar Yorkshire vowels rounded out by his Cambridge University education, rang with authority in the timber rafters.

This really is happening. I am getting married.

Her head was spinning.

Why does this feel like a dream I am going to wake up from?

The strains of the opening hymn sounded.

"Praise, my soul, the King of Heaven ... Ransomed, healed, restored, forgiven, Who like these His praise should sing ..."

As a new verse began and Max gently took her hand in his, Leilani came back to reality.

"Angels, help us to adore him …"

The last notes of the opening hymn died away, and the air seemed filled with a sacred silence. Leilani thought it was as if the congregation held a collective breath. No one coughed or shuffled.

Were the angels truly with them?

Bishop Thomas placed his hand over their joined hands and continued.

"Marriage is a sign of unity and loyalty which all should uphold and honor… No one should enter into it lightly or selfishly, but reverently and responsibly in the sight of Almighty God.

"Leilani and Maximus are now to enter this way of life. They will each give their consent to the other and make solemn vows…"

The bishop stared out into the congregation and his voice took on an extra layer of authority.

"First, I am required to ask anyone present who knows a reason why these persons may not lawfully marry, declare it now."

The sacred silence seemed to evaporate as Bishop Thomas gazed over the assembled throng, his dark eyebrows slightly contracted. Leilani felt as if the spell had broken, as feet shuffled nervously and a baby cried.

The bishop dropped his eyes back to his prayer book, ready to continue.

Then there was a loud cry from the back of the church.

"Stop! I know of due reason…"

Max whirled around as a heavy male tread thundered down the aisle.

The bishop's head jerked up from his prayer book.

The footsteps came to a sudden stop in front of him.

Aristide Laurent was standing beside her, a sheaf of documents in his hand.

The bishop stepped around Leilani to stand directly in front of

Laurent. She stared straight ahead, noticing for the first time the bridal flowers on the altar, white torch ginger, the passion flowers with their delicate purple centers, white native hibiscus, pikake jasmine and spicy scented orchids. She'd have to thank Malia for overseeing the flowers.

If she just kept looking at the flowers....

"You know of due cause, my son? State your case."

Aristide Laurent thrust the papers toward the Bishop, who still held the gold embossed Book of Common Prayer open in both hands.

"Take a look at these documents, Bishop. They prove Mr. Moeller has a wife in America. He is not free to wed."

He had spoken softly, too softly to reach the back of the church.

Leilani felt Max stiffen at her side. As Laurent had spoken, he'd barked a protest. "Damnation, man ..."

But as the Frenchman continued, Max subsided into guttural mutterings. Leilani suspected they were curses in his native tongue.

The Bishop set aside the prayer book on a lectern and took the packet of papers.

"Ladies and gentlemen, we'll be taking a ten-minute recess. Please stay in your seats."

And then all hell broke loose. The congregation rose, cried out, objected, queried...

Leilani glanced to where Queen Emma and Ani sat, in the same pew as Malia.

The bishop was standing back to make way for the King, flanked on each side by a retainer to steady his walk to the vestry, off the the altar. Then he turned to shepherd her and Max out.

The bishop was shepherding her and Max toward the vestry off the altar.

She stepped forward and took hold of his hand.

"Bishop. My mother and the queen should be included…"

The bishop signaled to Ezra Chance, who stood nearby, and whispered in his ear. He went to the two ladies—the official and unofficial dowagers of the realm—and ushered them in behind her.

Her shoulders erect, her back ramrod straight, she followed the bishop out of the chancel, not once daring to look at Max or Aristide.

Twenty-three

"I am so sorry, Lani. I failed you. And so did Lot. I'll never forgive myself. Or him for that matter. How could he not have known?"

Ani's voice was weak, but her coal-black eye blazed like a hot ember from the white pillows that supported her drooping head.

Leilani reached across the starched linen and took Ani's gnarled hand between hers, cushioning the worn palm, stroking the fan of wrinkled age-spotted fingers.

Ani had walked in the door and straight into bed when they'd returned from the cathedral yesterday, and terror had not left Leilani's mind in the hours since. With her last wish thwarted, Ani seemed to have given up. The fury in her eyes was the only sign of vitality left in her fragile body. The pillows swallowed her up. Her breathing was too rapid and shallow, and she refused to eat.

"Please, Ani. Don't berate yourself. It's all over now. It won't kill us. Either of us. It was an embarrassment, that's all. My reputation will survive. No one will remember in a year or two."

The burning inside belied her brave words. It was taking all her strength not to burst into tears and weep all over Ani's immaculate linen. But why? Because she also had to admit to a dark sense of relief. It wasn't decent to admit it yet, but she knew the day would come when she'd be grateful for the reprieve.

Ani squeezed her hand, as if calling her back from her daydreaming.

"Your reputation? That's what is so unfair. He publicly humiliated you. And you've done nothing to deserve that."

Maybe not. But she'd admitted to no one that Aristide had tried to warn her, and she'd been too proud to listen.

She felt her cheeks heat at the memory. She'd been more than proud. She'd been arrogant, filled up with the idea he was acting out of sour grapes. The memory of that encounter was as privately humiliating as what had happened yesterday.

She returned her attention to Ani. Her hairline was damp to her touch. Deep grooves snaked across her forehead, but the old lady took another breath and spoke again.

"To have the ceremony interrupted like that—with the king and Queen Emma present as well—it doesn't bear thinking about."

She convulsed in a paroxysm of coughing.

Lani drew her hand around Ani's shoulders and hauled her more fully upright so she could catch her breath. Her flannelette nightdress was clammy. She probably had a temperature, and she weighed no more than a sparrow.

As she settled her back against the pillows, Leilani's mind flicked back to the mortifying scene in the cathedral vestry. Bishop Thomas in episcopal robes and embroidered stole, carefully examining Aristide's documents while everyone else stood around him in silence. Max's waxen complexion told her before the bishop or anyone else spoke that he was expecting damnation from their contents. He avoided meeting her eye, staring at the wall, his shoulders slumped forward. She'd never seen him so dejected.

The bishop handed the pages on to the king without speaking, and when Lot had finished with them, he silently passed them to Queen Emma, his face stern. It seemed they were all too stunned to say anything.

Emma was the first to speak. She shuffled through, reading, and then looked up and prodded an accusing finger into Max's braided chest.

"It's always the same. The women left to suffer, isn't it, sir? Are you in your right mind? You've already got a wife, as these papers make plain. So what are you doing, collecting another? You've perpetrated this fiction not just on our dear daughter, but on the Kamehameha royal line. You've sullied the friendship and trust offered here over many years."

She turned to Lot. "Lot Kapuaiwa. As your loyal subject and dearest friend, I request in the authority vested in you as Kamehameha V, you strip this man of all the honors bestowed by this kingdom. Any suggestion of further relationship with him is unconscionable."

Kamehameha V dropped his head to his chest with a deep sigh.

When he lifted it again, lines of deep grief scored his cheeks.

"She's right, Moeller. There's no place for you here. Please go."

"But… but… I can explain…" Max was standing his ground, his hands clenched in fists at his sides, his jaw determined.

The Bishop stepped forward. "I am sorry, sir, but no explanation can absolve you of this deception before Almighty God. Those vows you were preparing to make. You must understand, they are not just before a human audience, but before the face of God. Please. Obey your sovereign and leave now."

Max turned to her then, his face a white mask. "I am so sorry, Leilani. I did not intend for it to end this way."

He shot her a desperate look of appeal, turned, and walked out.

Shaking off her painful daydreaming, Leilani angled a bright smile at Ani, sunk in her pillows. "That was quite a scene in the vestry, wasn't it? And wasn't Emma magnificent? Now there's a woman you want on your side. Now wonder she and Queen Victoria get on so well."

She punched her words with cheeky brio, though inside she felt so bruised it amazed her she could still stand upright.

Ani's lips quirked up in a ghost of a smile.

"That's better.. Now you put all this upset behind you. I'm going to bring you some tea, and then you need to rest."

Twenty-four

There was no triumph for Aristide in his victory. When he'd looked across the unadorned vestry and saw Leilani's stricken face in the light cast from the clerestory windows, he wondered if it might have been better to leave her to marry Max Moeller, rather than witness the destruction he'd caused.

She was biting her lower lip, as if willing herself not to cry. When she'd arrived at the altar, she'd thrown back the wispy muslin veil that hung from a blossom-wreathed band. After Max left, she'd flicked it back down over her face.

He'd saved her from marrying a bigamist, but at the cost of public humiliation. She was a proud woman. He was pretty sure she'd hate him for life.

She left via the main doors, her face concealed.

He braced his shoulders and strode out after her, unrepentant.

He'd come here to secure her for himself, he acknowledged that. But he'd realized weeks ago he was out of his league, and he'd then resolved to protect her in any way he could.

Well, he'd done that, and now he could go home. Resume his old life. Try to forget all about Hawaii and Leilani Manolo.

There was just one more thing he needed to see to before he departed.

***

"Titus, old chap. I'll be out of your hair sooner than I realized. I've booked today to return to California on the Moses Taylor departing Christmas Eve. Sir John wanted me back by the end of January, so I'll be home two weeks early."

Titus looked up from his desk, his eyebrows lifted in surprise.

"That's a shame, Aristide. I was getting used to having you around."

He gave him a wry grin.

"But I understand. Maybe there's not much to hold you here any longer."

"Quite right, Titus. I've finished my business here. There's just one last thing…"

He explained to Titus what he had in mind.

"Can we put a proposal to Hector? Max is a good as dead here. He won't get any patronage from the king, so why not try and help Honey along? If I could achieve that, I could leave feeling the trip had been worthwhile."

They sat together late into the night, plotting and scheming, preparing a report for the senator on the latest happenings and suggesting his next steps. Titus would telegraph him their proposal first thing in the morning.

"You've been a great friend, Titus. You really have."

"Just sorry it didn't work out better for you, Aristide, but that's life. The ancients plainly got it wrong when they told us *Fortuna Fortes Juvat.*' 'Fortune favors the bold, or the brave.' This time it clearly didn't. Now, how about a nightcap before you turn in? And you can help me with one last conundrum before you go."

"Oh? What's that?" Aristide glanced up, his spirits lifting at his friend's jesting tone.

"You're the ladies' man. How am I going to get that lovely Malia Manolo to marry an old fellow like me?"

Aristide broke into a delighted laugh.

"Given my current track record, I'm plainly not the one to ask. But if I were the Romeo you seem to think I am, then I'd suggest one thing. Show her you take her seriously. She is one accomplished young woman. She's consistently underestimated by those around her. Show her you understand that and watch her flourish…"

Twenty-five

Leilani was leaving Ani's room, having settled her in for an afternoon nap, when she felt a vice-like grip on her upper arm.

"You never told me Hector de Vile was your father," a man's voice snarled.

Her head jerked back as she attempted to wrench herself free.

"Max," she cried. "What are you doing here?"

Concealed in the doorway down the hall from Ani's room, he'd waited for his opportunity to pounce. Her arm pinched from the unyielding clamp of his meaty hands.

"Let. Me. Go." She turned to face him, her jaw set, her words spitting and determined.

"You're not welcome here, Max. You know that. The king wants nothing more to do with you. So go."

"Not until I find out just what kind of scheming little hussy you are."

She gave him an incredulous stare.

"What are you talking about? Do you think I'd have presented myself at the altar if I'd had any inkling? What do you take me for?"

"Then how did that Frenchman get his hands on private information? There are only a few people in the world who knew about Johanna, and Hector de Vile was one of them. Now I discover he's your father?" He spat the words out. "Why didn't you tell me that?"

"Because it's none of your business. And I have nothing to do with him."

She glared at Max, her eyes cold.

"I have nothing to do with Aristide Laurent, either, so don't blame me for your woes. What? Did you think it was all right to marry when your first wife was still alive?"

Max shrugged. "The Hawaiians did it with impunity before they discovered religion. Now they've got all holier than thou about it."

She shook her arm again to loosen his clutches, and this time he let go.

She stepped away from him.

"That just shows what you really think of us. And what about the wife you already have?"

"Johanna is quite happy where she is. I pay her bills. She's not concerned."

"And what about any children we might have had? How would that play out? You know it obsessed Lot—the idea of adding to the family line. And then to find they were not legitimate heirs? Honestly, Max, I don't know you."

His lips curled in a knowing sneer. "Well, seeing as to how you're not a true Manolo anyway, I don't see what difference it makes. I obviously picked the wrong sister. I should have focused on the blind fool. They'd have been happy to see her mated."

Leilani tensed, unwilling to believe what her ears had just heard. And then with a whack she'd perfected as a tomboy playing with Kaleo's friends, she slapped Max across the cheek. Loud. Broad. Stinging and true.

"Get out of here," she screamed. "Get out this minute or I'll call the palace guards. You're not fit to wipe Malia's shoes."

She looked down the hall. The commotion she'd raised had already attracted attention. One of Lot's red-coated footmen was trotting toward her at a fast clip.

"If you're not gone in five seconds, he'll propel you out that door faster than Mauna Loa spews lava."

Max glanced around at the sound of approaching feet.

"All right. All right. But you haven't heard the last of me."

Twenty-six

"How are you, Ani? We're worried about you."

It was early evening and Malia had joined Leilani at Ani's bedside. She'd refused anything more than a thin vegetable soup for dinner. She squeezed her rheumy eyes shut at Leilani's solicitations.

"I'm fine, girls. My daughters, my *ka'u mau kaikumāhine*. My time has come, that's all."

"Don't say that, Ani. Please. We want you here with us for many years yet."

"Ahhh. I've run out of mana, girls. Plain run out of the breath of life. Max took the last of it from me."

"Oh Ani, no! It's not true. That man can't hurt any of us anymore."

Leilani shuddered as she thought of the confrontation earlier in the day and hoped that was true.

"You know, I sent him packing earlier today. He came here asking questions about Hector de Vile, Ani. Most odd. It reminded me we never really finished our conversation about my father. If you're up to it, could we continue with that now?"

Ani brightened, as if the idea of talking about the old days was exactly what she needed

"Ahh, Lilolilo… a fine man. De Vile? A bold fellow, I'll give him that. Your mother was under his spell."

"Max blames Hector for his bigamy being exposed. Could that be right?"

Ani nodded. "It could be. Hector's spies were everywhere. That's why it was so surprising he never found out what Archie did to him."

"What do you mean?"

Leilani's stomach sank. She shivered with foreboding. Was there something else dark and deadly in her family's past that she didn't know about?

Ani pursed her lips.

"What did Archie do to Hector, Ani?"

Is taking our mother away enough of an injury, or is there more to the story?

Ani's jaw had taken on a mutinous cast. Leilani sighed and stroked the back of her hand.

"I'm old enough to know now, Ani. Especially with what I've just been through. If you really believe you're 'running out of mana,' you owe it to us to tell us before you join Lilolilo in Hawaiian heaven. I don't want to find out secrets after you're gone."

Ani made her characteristic throaty sound of disapproval.

"Your father's a proud man, Leilani. A domineering man. He was too demanding for me. He walked over anyone who got in his way. But your mother, Abigail? He enthralled her. And she was a match for him, in terms of her strength.

"She wasn't a walkover. My goodness, they had their arguments, but she captivated Hector too. They were both charismatic, bubbling over with spirit, risk takers. They pushed one another to the limits and beyond, all the time."

She sighed, and a tear trickled down her face from her blind eye. She continued, unaware she was weeping.

"Everything might have ended differently if they'd been willing to do things Archie's way, who knows? But they couldn't or wouldn't do that."

She swiped her face, noticing its wetness.

"Those friends of hers—the consul who died a couple of months back—they were in on it."

Leilani's heart jumped. "Cyrus? Cyrus and Misty?"

Cyrus and Misty May had been like godparents to her in the absence of her own parents, and their murder-suicide a few months back had devastated her. She'd had suspicions de Vile bore some responsibility for it, though she had no clue how.

"Yes. Them. They'd arranged to get married on Maui, and Abigail and Hector were going as the best man and bridesmaid. They secretly set it up as a double ceremony—your mother and Hector were wed by the same celebrant at the same time."

"Oh. I never knew that. Misty never said…"

She felt that familiar sense of overwhelming grief. All the conversations she'd never had, and it was too late for them now.

Why haven't I asked these questions before now? Has the cloak of silence encouraged us to leave it alone?

Her voice cracked. She struggled to continue. "I wish I'd known this earlier."

The old Ani, the one who'd presided over her childhood, would have barked back something like, *What difference would that make? She's dead.*

Leilani shuddered at the internal voice that chided her.

But this Ani, the one lying quietly on the pillows before her, said nothing like that.

Instead, she rolled her hand over the top of Leilani's and squeezed it gently.

"Archie swore us all to total secrecy, Leilani. You'll see why in a minute. And as time went on, everyone who was in on it was too frightened to talk about it."

Leilani trembled.

"What else could there possibly be?"

Ani searched her face with her burning black eyes. She reached out and ran her withered hand down Leilani's cheek with a tenderness that left her breathless. When had Ani ever been this gentle and loving? Leilani felt as if a wellspring of love that had been blocked for a lifetime was gushing forth. Tears flowed down her face, but she was hiccupping with laughter.

"Tell me. The suspense is killing me."

Ani laughed too, and for a brief moment she looked like the Ani of her youth.

Then her face grew serious again.

"Archie wasn't satisfied with dissolving the marriage and turning Abigail over to Lilolilo. He wanted to ensure your father made no claim on you children. He couldn't abide the thought of anything messy, and he knew Hector was a determined man, with a strong sense of responsibility for what was his…. Protecting you from his interference became Archie's life purpose.

"He heard of some complication in Hector's own family, something to do with Hector's father's estate. I don't know all the details. Something about Hector being in line for an inheritance if he'd married and had children by a certain age. That aroused Archie's suspicions about Hector's motives."

She laid her hand on top of Leilani's, and the younger woman felt it tremor as she continued.

"This is the hardest part of all to admit to, Leilani. But it has to be told. You twins were a bit over a year old. Malia was just a baby, a few months old, when the measles epidemic hit Maui.

"You all got terribly ill; Abigail and all you children. As you know, that's when Malia's sight was affected. When your mother died, Archie saw his chance. So many people dying, too many to keep track of, it was a dreadful time."

Ani's voice slowed. She sank lower into her pillows.

Malia leaned over, her brow creased with concern. "If this is too much, Ani, we can leave it for tonight and continue in the morning. Don't exhaust yourself."

"No, no, I want to continue." The old woman took in a series of rasping breaths. "I've got to finish."

Malia stroked her arm, and Ani resumed in a hoarse whisper. "Archie announced to the world that Abbie and the twins had died in the epidemic. He had funeral caskets made for all of you. Hector heard about it—his ship was in port. He came to the funeral, even though Archie tried to put him off. He saw everything. He left Hawaii the next day, and we never saw him again.

"Matthew died in a shark attack not long after. And life just continued as usual. You weren't the only children we were looking after, you remember. Archie opened a dormitory wing for all the children in the village who'd lost their parents. If anyone asked, you were Abbie and Matthew's children, being cared for by their grandfather. No one thought anything of it.

"So that's how it was. I don't know how de Vile found out the rest of it, after all these years. But he did."

Ani yawned, and fell into an exhausted silence. Within minutes she was again fast asleep.

***

Malia, watching the conversation in tender silence, leaned over to stroke Ani's slick forehead.

"She's breathing heavily, and she's too hot. I think we should call the doctor again. We don't want to take risks with her."

She walked around to Leilani's side of the bed and lightly massaged her shoulders.

"It's good that she's asleep, though. How about you, Lani? That was a shocking story. Are you all right?"

Leilani screwed her body around to face her half-sister.

Her hands went to her mouth, as if to suppress a cry.

"Oh Malia, can you believe it?" she whispered through her fingers.

"Archie held our funeral! He's already got us dead and buried! Long ago! I can't believe it! That must be such bad *laki*. Bad luck. No wonder everything's been going wrong!"

Malia stroked her long warm fingers down the back of her neck.

"I can understand you feel upset about it, Lani, but look at it this way. It was really only theater, wasn't it?"

Leilani shook her head vehemently. "No. No! It was more than that! It's a curse. No wonder when Archie died everything started going wrong. It's payback for his wrong actions, and we're suffering for it. He did wrong to us and to our father. How could he?"

She brought her hands to her eyes and covered her face for a long minute, mute in her protest.

Her raven-black hair had fallen over her face, and she pushed it away angrily.

"I was so horrible to Aristide when he tried to talk to me about de Vile. I was so arrogant. And de Vile! He saved me from a bigamous marriage, after the way I've treated him! I wouldn't even talk to him, and yet he's helped me."

She threw Malia a despairing stare.

"I thought I knew it all. And I know nothing!"

She shook her head, her eyes desolate.

"I've behaved badly to everyone who cared."

She buried her head in her hands and sobbed.

***

A long time later, when she dried her eyes and the sisters had eaten some of Ani's thin soup, nursing plates on their knees as they kept a vigil at Ani's bedside, Leilani tapped Malia's arm.

"What am I going to do to fix this, my wise Sis? Regardless of what sort of old rogue the senator might be, Archie treated the senator wretchedly. He deserves the traditional Hawaiian reconciliation, like the old people used to offer. I feel it in my bones. For our sakes, as much as his."

Hawaiian tradition contended that breaking spiritual laws or *kapu* angered the gods and resulted in illness and misfortune. However, prayer and forgiveness "untied" the bad fortune.

"That sounds like a good idea," Malia said. "But we've still got a ways to go before we'll be free to do that. Let's not fret about it now. This business with Max has knocked Ani out. She needs to get better first. Then you'll have time to consider what to do about de Vile."

Leilani was momentarily blinded by tears. Darling, wise, perceptive Malia, couldn't, wouldn't see it. She was hoping, praying, for the impossible. Ani's time had come, as the old woman had insisted it would.

Ani died in her sleep hours after their last conversation, and Leilani couldn't shake a deep sense of responsibility for the veteran lady's passing. The mess of the aborted wedding was too much for her, she told herself.

If she hadn't mismanaged everything—caring too much about the blasted water, refusing to listen to Aristide, ignoring warning signs that Max was not what he presented himself to be, being ignorant and hasty—then Ani would still be alive.

The funeral in the Cathedral chapel only days after she'd proceeded down the aisle in her wedding dress, full of hope, passed before her like a bad dream. Sunk deep in sorrow and regret, she'd barely raised her eyes from Ani's casket during the prolonged formalities.

But when she looked up, what had she seen, but Honey Cleveland, nestled cozily in the pew between Aristide and Titus. Blurred by her tears, she jerked her gaze straight back to Ani's casket. Clearly he'd already moved on, and who could blame him?

From the first news of Ani's death, Malia had read Leilani's distress and quietly slipped into the role of lead mourner. Leilani recoiled from the pity and disapproval she read in faces around her. Did they whisper that the aborted wedding had been the death of Ani? She guessed they did.

And what of Hector de Vile? She felt less convinced she'd done wrong by him, but she harbored a conviction still that she had to right the wrongs done in her family's name. That was the Hawaiian way.

At the reading of Ani's last will and testament as she lay in state in the "English Church"—the popular name for the Pro Cathedral—they'd discovered she wanted her body returned to Maui for burial near the place of her birth. For Leilani, the request was a relief and an escape. She insisted on accompanying her back home, leaving Malia and Titus to manage any family business in Honolulu.

Twenty-seven

The old Front Street house on Lahaina's waterfront seemed as familiar to her now as it was in her earliest memory, of being enfolded into Ani's lap as a sniffling three-year-old dumped by a wave. She remembered what it felt like to have Ani's arms around her, as strong and reassuring as the forest's maile vine, revered for fragrant funeral and wedding leis.

That long-ago day, her pride hurt more than her grazed knee, she recalled, because Kaleo laughed at her. They'd spent their first ten years in this house where Archie and Connie had started out as missionaries.

And now she smelt again the salty air that blew in from Lahaina Roads, the deep safe harbor channel off the town where hundreds of whalers and other ships anchored for safe shelter. It was from here that her sea captain father would have first come ashore and seen her free-spirited mother, a famed Lahaina beauty.

Dr. Hank Freeman, the genial doctor cum preacher who now occupied "Archie's" house with his family, knew all about the dramas of the last week—an aborted wedding, a sudden funeral—and welcomed her with open arms. The venerable home was the oldest and best-known domestic dwelling in town, a center of social activity, its occupants well used to accommodating random guests, whether they were visiting royals or rogues.

And as she sat on the first-floor veranda and looked out to the horizon, she felt a curling sense of peace for the first time in weeks. The tightness across her shoulders relaxed a fraction as she inhaled the marine breeze and watched the downy seagrass heads dance.

As she gazed through the expansive windows at the front of the house, windows that faced the prevailing ocean breeze and kept the house cool, she recalled the many times she'd watched for what was happening down on the beach. She'd spy Kaleo out there and run off to join him and his friends; the boys trying to lose her as often as not.

This had been an auspicious place, with its thick lava and coral block walls that protected a little girl from the monsters lurking in her imagination. Airy, too, with the rough-hewn timber rafters that framed the high ceilings.

The Freemans still lived largely as they had fifteen years ago, doing most of their cooking and household laundry in the outside kitchen and fire pit in the rear yard hedged with bananas, breadfruit, figs and grapes that provided food through the year.

But as her eyes roamed up the street, a chill replaced the tiny wisps of calm that had settled in her spirit. Only a few blocks away stood Kamehameha's old palace, the scene of their staged twin funeral. Her spine tingled. Was Hector grieving, that night many years ago, when he'd learned his wife and children had died?

Or was he affronted at being out-maneuvered by a cunning missionary old enough to be his father? Was their feud an inevitable clash of two imperious wills intent on wielding power—one in the carnal world, the other in the spiritual realm, and neither willing to cede to the other?

She felt a pain deep in her chest, and once again a sense of deep loss and sadness threatened to overwhelm her. So many questions she still didn't have answers to, nor did she have the drive or purpose to find them. Since Ani's death ten days ago, her world had closed in around her. She was in the deepest hole she'd ever been in in her life, and she didn't know how long it was going to take her to climb out of it.

Lahaina town had risen as one heart and offered Ani a royal farewell, her casket accompanied to the graveyard by ritual chants and hundreds of keening mourners. They'd given her a leave-taking loud and long enough to rouse the dead. And when the last shovelful of earth landed with a thud on her grave mound, Leilani turned back to the Freeman house with a sense of completion and asked herself, "What do I do next?"

***

Much later that night she was back in her favorite chair, gazing out to sea, drinking in the rhythm of the waves. A whisper as they surged in and then a hiss as they withdrew. The accompaniment to her childhood, the reassuring breath of the ocean.

The garden gate below clicked. Dr. Freeman's characteristic straw hat showed for a second, then passed out of view. Her host was home, probably returning from a house visit to a local patient. She heard his tread on the stairs, and then he'd drawn up a chair beside her.

"Leilani! I feel we've abandoned you! So much going on! We haven't been able to give you the attention we'd have liked. Do you have everything you need?"

Leilani looked into his kindly, angular face, his finely arched intelligent blue eyes full of concern, and laughed.

"Dr. Freeman, it couldn't be better. I need this quiet solitude more than anything. To sit here on your veranda and look back down the years… it's a balm for my soul."

Hank Freeman gave her a thoughtful smile. "I'm glad to hear it.

You've had a rough old time of it the last few weeks. You deserve some peace."

There was a natural pause, as they both sat gazing out to where the waves were breaking, a half moon rising on the dark gray line of the horizon.

"Look at that," said Dr. Freeman, his voice weighted with wonder. He let the moment gather its own awed silence, and then his voice came softly through the dark.

"Your times might have been turbulent, Leilani, but you know God's always in control, don't you? You've nothing to fear."

Her head tilted sharply. "In control, Dr. Freeman? Forgive me, but that's the priest speaking, surely? From where I sit, life could hardly feel any more out of control!"

She attempted to lighten the stinging comment with a laugh, but it came out sounding more like a sob.

He gazed at her, his face calm, his eyes gentle, his ear toward her, as if his sole purpose was to listen, and hers to talk.

And she couldn't help it. Everything she'd bottled up came out in a torrent.

"I came within a hair's breadth of marrying a man who already had a living wife. I scorned people who had only the best intentions toward me. And then I broke my darling Ani's heart. How could it get any worse?"

She drew in a gasping breath and despite her iron will, her lower lip trembled.

Dr Freeman allowed another long, restoring silence to settle before he replied.

"You broke Ani's heart, you say? How did you do that, might I ask?"

"She'd still be alive if she hadn't had such a big upset over the mess of a wedding. She was obsessed about seeing me 'settled,' as she saw it. And all her plans collapsed. She hated public humiliation. More than I do!" Again she tried to inject a joking tone and failed.

"I don't think her heart could take it. She was already ailing..."

Hank Freeman drew his chair very slightly closer to hers and leaned in to capture her eye.

"She was ailing, you're right. Over the summer, while you were away, she came to Maui for a break and I attended her. It's not breaking any patient confidentiality now to tell you I knew then she probably would not live to see Christmas. Her heart could not do the work, Leilani. It's as simple as that. Wedding or no wedding."

Leilani's hand clutched at her throat. Tears spilled down her cheeks.

"What... what are you saying?"

"Ani knew she was dying, Leilani. I didn't conceal my diagnosis from her. She wouldn't have wanted me to."

He gave her another long minute to regain control of her emotions.

"It's not your fault she died when she did, Leilani. I believe having you back home extended her life by a few weeks at least. Maybe months. She was holding on for you to come back."

She could hold the dam back no longer.

"Oh, Dr. Freeman."

The tears overflowed, and this time there was no staunching them.

She wept for Ani, and her unrealized passion for Lilolilo. She cried for Aristide, her staunch friend—and maybe more—whom she'd spurned. She cried for herself, prematurely buried, ruined now and lost at sea, with no idea where safe harbor lay. And she cried for the father she'd never known, cruelly deceived over the death of his children.

Unperturbed by her sobs, Dr. Freeman handed her a handful of crisp white handkerchiefs, and left her to it with a simple "Cry, girlie. It'll do you good."

She cried until she was dry, until there were no tears to release.

Then she just sat, numb and bleary-eyed, until a thin rose-pink line on the horizon told her the dawn was coming soon.

The moon had risen and gone again as she'd hugged herself in grief. But the waves had not ceased their rhythmic secret whispering. The galaxies still wheeled overhead.

And as she rose, dog tired and heading for her lace coverlet bed, she knew with a spring in her heart, that just like nature around her, there'd be no arresting her momentum, either.

Twenty-eight

"A lot has happened while you were on Maui. Want to hear about it?" Honey twirled the salmon-rose parasol that matched her newest dress and gave Leilani a conspiratorial wink.

Leilani bristled and then reminded herself she'd resolved on the boat back from Lahaina to change her ways and suffer fools a little more generously than she had in the past.

Not that Honey's a fool. Far from it. She knows Max better than I ever did.

She'd docked just on sunset, still exhausted from her all-nighter. She'd hugged Malia and made her excuses.

"Let's leave talking till the morning. I'll cope a lot better after a good night's sleep."

Malia had stolen out early, she presumed to go riding. And she hadn't been up long when Honey tapped on the door, suggesting they share a coffee in a tone which left no room for rebuff.

She'd quickly scooped her bed-tumbled hair into a tidy knot at the back of her neck and followed Honey to a utilitarian harborside stall which sold coffee, juices, and fresh fruit like pineapple and coconut.

She perched on a stool opposite Honey and grinned. "Well,

Honey, you know the old saying about 'It's an ill wind that blows nobody any good.' I guess that awful Max business was good for you. There's no way your father will foist you off on him now."

Honey tinkled her girlish laugh. "So right there, sister. But the downside is neither do we have much chance of getting our shares back. But more of that later. Tell me, how have you been?"

Leilani darted a suspicious glare her way and then quickly softened it. The young heiress-to-nothing looked genuinely concerned, her eyebrows drawn together, her eyes shining with sympathy.

"Oh, pretty much as you might imagine. It's been hard. Terribly hard. First the humiliation of the non-wedding. And then Ani dying. It was like being shot twice in the chest at point-blank range."

Honey shook her head vigorously. "No one thinks the worse of you because of the wedding, Leilani. Truly. They despise Max for what he did, but they don't blame you. Of course you wouldn't have got that far if you'd known he had a wife. And how could you know? It was a closely guarded secret."

Leilani looked up, suddenly curious.

"You didn't know?"

"Give me credit, sister! If I'd had any inkling, I promise I would have warned you somehow. It was as much a surprise to me as to anyone. What a stinker he is."

"Then how did Aristide find out? I mean… I feel like the skies have fallen in, and I haven't picked up the pieces yet."

"You should ask him yourself, Leilani."

Leilani's cheeks grew hot.

"I don't imagine he'd want to talk to me. I was awful to him the last couple of times we met. More than awful. An absolute witch. I'm embarrassed at how horrible I was."

Honey shrugged. "He's pretty forgiving. And I don't think it's any secret that Senator de Vile provided the documents."

She eyed Leilani, as if searching for something.

"What. What is it?" Leilani prickled under her assessing gaze.

"As far as I understand it, he did it to save you from the embarrassment of a bigamous marriage. Don't ask me why he should care…"

Leilani's skin flushed again, and she had the panicky urge to change the subject.

"So where does that leave Max and Diamond Sugar?"

Honey called to the bright-eyed teenager who was staffing the cabin. "Another juice here, sweetie. Do you want anything more, Leilani?"

She shook her head and waited.

When Honey had taken a few sips of her fresh juice, she paused.

"Max and Diamond? He's the kiss of death in the kingdom now, no question. There's no way the king will do any business with Diamond while he's a shareholder, and he knows it. He shamed the king's friendship, and no one does that and gets away with it. I guess he'll quit his shares for what he can get for them. And you can bet no one will pay full price."

She gave a muffled laugh behind her hand and leaned forward to whisper. "He tried to get in before my father heard about the scandal and give them back at half price, but Dad wasn't having it. We probably couldn't even raise the money for half, anyway."

"So what's going to happen, do you think?"

Honey examined her fingernails.

"I think Senator de Vile might take up Max's share. One thing's for sure. The king will never lease water to Diamond while Max is still in the company. Not now."

Twenty-nine

He'd come to say goodbye. Aristide reminded himself of that fact as he strode across the lawn to the Manolo house on the palace grounds. His heart thumped hard against his ribs. The pain in his chest reminded him this farewell would be the hardest of his life.

He'd thought of little else but Leilani's stricken face when he'd produced the papers proving Max's bigamy in the cathedral vestry. He'd have done anything in the world to save her from that embarrassment—except allow her to go through with the ceremony knowing what he did.

And the only other time he'd seen her since that awful day was at Ani's funeral. She'd glanced to where he sat in the pew with Honey and Titus, but her face was so frozen he couldn't tell if she'd registered anything.

The house manager answered his knock promptly and took him straight into the breakfast room where Leilani held a coffee cup to a pale, drawn face.

When she saw him in the doorway, her expression dissolved into the same mask-like blankness she'd displayed at the funeral. She seemed a long way away from the sunny breakfast room, with the early morning rays slanting onto finely woven floor mats. He stepped forward warily and made a slight bow.

"Leilani. I wanted to come and see you before I go." He hesitated, uncertain of how to continue.

Her eyes flicked to his face and then slowly roamed his body, as if surveying unfamiliar territory, or committing something to memory. The quick-witted, effervescent woman he'd known was nowhere in evidence.

She was wearing a dark navy-blue dress with black cuffs. Perched in her hair was a mourning cockade copied from Queen Victoria, with three sprouting feathers—black, white and red. The dark blue of the dress sapped vitality from her normally vibrant complexion.

Of course. She was in mourning. How stupid of him to overlook that.

"Are you all right? Do you want to sit down?"

She'd risen when the manager had announced his arrival, and now she stood at the table, bracing herself on its wooden edge.

"I'm fine." Brisk. Business-like. Emotionless. "Did you say you're going somewhere?"

"Yes. Back to Vino d'Oro. To Sir John and the winery. I always was only on a brief holiday here."

Her eyes flickered, and took on a distant cast. For a moment he wondered if she remembered where she was.

"Of course. That's right."

She stood frozen, an elegant bird deciding whether to stay in camouflage or make her escape. Fight or flight.

"And when do you leave?"

"In a few days. On Christmas Eve. On the Moses Taylor. The steamship that does the mail run to San Fran. You know the one." He was babbling now. "I quite like the idea of having a quiet Christmas at sea. Just me and the flying fish."

He gave her a sad smile. She stared absently into his face.

Shut up or she really will think you've lost your mind.

She turned then and gestured toward the French doors leading to the outside deck.

"Let's go outside. Do you mind? I find it hard being cooped up inside these days. I don't know why."

Without awaiting a response, she turned and led the way out to the sheltered lanai. Beams of sunlight streamed through a lattice, covered with a sweet-smelling native vine with small white flowers. As soon as she sat and breathed in the garden freshness, the stiffness in her shoulders eased.

"Aristide, I wanted to thank you for all that you've done." Her voice was soft and melodious, with no sign of the anxiety she'd shown a few moments ago. She glanced up, and saw that he was about to interrupt her.

She raised her hand with a hint of the old imperious Leilani. "No. Say nothing. I'm not finished. I was awful to you the last time we met. So rude. And if I'd taken more notice, we could have avoided that terrible showdown in the cathedral. All my fault, that."

He did jump in then. "When I spoke to you, Leilani, I only had a suspicion. I had no documentation, as you so correctly pointed out. And I can understand you wouldn't consider me the most objective of sources…" He gave her a wry smile, but still she looked past him.

"As far as it being your fault. That is total nonsense. Max bears responsibility for that mess. He deserves everything that's coming to him."

She looked at him then, as if her interest had suddenly been piqued.

"And what is coming to him? Businesswise, I mean. Honey says he's the kiss of death for Diamond Sugar. Is that true?"

He nodded. "From what Titus says. He's been talking with the king while you were away, trying to clean up the mess. His Royal

Highness won't give Diamond any water as long as Max is there, so he's being forced out. Titus knows the details better than I do."

Leilani nodded, as if satisfied with his answer. "I was wrong for getting so upset about you talking to the senator too. If you hadn't had that connection… I hate to think what dilemma I might be facing. Even worse than the one I am in now."

She'd turned to look out over the gardens, and he had a few moments to secretly memorize her strong-willed, beautiful face.

One last time. He'd commit it to memory forever.

Even in this subdued mood her brown eyes had a deep sparkle, and her finely sculpted mouth quirked up at the corners, as if she could still find something irresistibly funny about the world.

He'd always remember her like this, poised and lovely, if a little sad.

"You're not going to Queen Emma's Christmas fete? She has one every year to raise money for the hospital."

The sudden change of topic startled him.

"The queen's fete?" He couldn't hide his amusement. "Can't say I've received my invitation, Leilani. I'm obviously not on the priority list."

She shot a sharp glance his way.

"Are you making fun of me?"

"Just a little." He leaned closer to her.

"I didn't have a good understanding of how things were when I came here, Leilani. I know you explained when we became friends, but it's helped a lot to visit. I understand a lot better, now. We inhabit different worlds, you and I. You have a role here in the kingdom I was only barely aware of. You've carried out your part magnificently and it's not your fault it didn't work out. The people who were advising you—yes, the king, and your poor Ani—they share most of the responsibility. They were grasping at straws to save a dynasty."

She fixed her deep liquid eyes on him.

"I'm very sorry it's turned out like it has, Aristide. I wish we could start over again, and make it all come out differently."

He shook his head in a gentle, sorrowful movement.

"That's just the thing, Leilani. We've been here before, haven't we? You need to be here for the sugar and your family. And I must get back to my work at Vino d'Oro."

He stood to leave.

"I don't regret coming to Hawaii for one minute. I like to think I helped save you from a disaster that might have ruined your life. And from what Titus says, you'll be happy with what he and Malia have been organizing while you were away. You have a lot to look forward to here, Leilani. Don't give up just yet."

He stepped back from the chair he'd occupied and turned toward the garden.

If he didn't leave right now he wouldn't be able to maintain this gentlemanly act, this smooth composure, any longer. He had such pain in his chest he wouldn't have been surprised if he'd looked down and seen a knife handle sticking out of it.

He glanced back once and gave her a mock salute.

"Have a wonderful Christmas, Leilani."

Then he was gone.

***

She sat frozen in her chair, unable to move, to call out, to do anything but watch as Aristide's lithe, muscled back receded across the blindingly green lawn.

Leaving her.

On the Moses Taylor.

In a few days. She probably wouldn't see him ever again.

"I quite like the idea of having a quiet Christmas at sea. Just me and the flying fish."

Did he really say that? Was he really going?

She had a lump in her throat like a stone, so round and hard she couldn't swallow.

He'd had it with her. She'd chosen Max, more fool her. And though he'd been so gentlemanly in the way he'd treated her, and so generous in protecting her from herself, he was moving on, and that's what she had to do too.

Her legs were stiff blocks of wood as she rose from the chair and turned to go inside.

She heard a strong, gay voice calling.

"Lani! Lani! We've got to talk!" And Malia, her dear, precious, clever Malia, bounded up the steps and engulfed her in a hug that smelled of lemongrass and patchouli.

"We've had such a time of it, Leilani. But before I get to that, how was Maui? And did everything go fine with Ani's interment?"

"Absolutely wonderfully. They treated her like a royal. She'd be thrilled. All of Lahaina and beyond turned out. It was magnificent. Just like the old days." She grinned. "Of course, I don't remember the old days. But that's what people said."

She gathered Malia to her side, gestured to the chair beside her. "Come and sit down."

Her sister was in a deep violet day dress with black cuffs which suited her creamy complexion. Something had changed in Malia. She carried herself with an authority Leilani hadn't noticed before.

"I had a lovely stay at Dr. Freeman's and I had a great talk with him. He told me something you must know, too. Ani knew her end was coming, because she had a bad turn when she was on Maui last summer and they called in Dr. Freeman. She had congestive heart failure, he says. He told her her heart wouldn't last much longer. He thought at the time he saw her she only had only five to six weeks."

Malia gazed at her in wonder. "And here we were trying to jolly her along, wanting to believe she had a few more years. Maybe not you, but I was certainly guilty of that. And she never let on."

Leilani nodded, and said quietly, "No, she didn't."

She punched Malia lightly on the arm. "But tell me what's been happening here? Aristide says you've been busy with the king?"

Malia's brow furrowed. "Aristide? Have you seen him?"

Leilani gestured vaguely to the lawn. "Oh, I've had a very busy morning. You don't know the half of it. I've seen Honey and Aristide already."

Her lips felt stiff, but she gave Malia her best smile.

"He was just here. Came to say goodbye. I suppose you know he's booked to leave on the Moses Taylor on Christmas Eve?"

Malia nodded. "I had heard. And you're OK with that?"

Leilani's heart pinched, and she thought of the old story of Pinocchio Connie used to read to them, with its stern admonitions about lying. Would her nose grow right out of her face?

She shrugged. "I guess. Not much I can do about it."

Malia's mouth twisted into a curious grimace. "I don't know... It depends on what you want..."

"It's not what I want. It's what needs doing." She surprised herself with the hard inflection of her words.

Malia latched right on to her.

"What you need is to come and talk to Titus. Then you might be in a better position to decide on that..."

Thirty

They found Titus on his deck as usual. Malia's two dogs lazed happily at his feet. He looked up from the papers he was working on and when he spotted her and Leilani coming through the beach gate he jumped up, plainly delighted. Malia's heart leapt in response. They'd only been apart a short time, but she never got over the charge of surprised pleasure she felt at seeing him again.

"Leilani! So good to have you home. I understand from Malia you had a sleep-in this morning—and much deserved I'm sure it was, too."

He glanced to Malia and gave her shoulders an affectionate squeeze as he pecked her on both cheeks.

"Can I get you fresh coffee?"

"I seem to have drunk nothing else today, but sure, why not," said Leilani with a grin. "At least there's no danger I'll drop off in the middle of talking business."

Titus left them to get coffee, and Leilani leaned down and fussed over the dogs, ruffling their necks and crooning to them, before shooting a quizzical look Malia's way. "They seem awfully at home here. Been spending a bit of time here while I've been away, have you?"

Malia stroked Kāne's neck. "Oh, I missed you so much, dear Sis," she teased. "I had to fill the gap somehow."

"Well, I'm very glad you found someone with integrity to do it with. Unlike me."

She pulled a face. "I'm never going to live that one down, am I?"

"You'll surprise yourself," said Malia. "Don't you worry."

Titus returned with fresh coffee. He hesitated, about to pour and pass the first cup. "Hot and black. That's how you like it, right?"

Leilani nodded. "Tell me. How's Lot's health? And what's his thinking on the water now Max is out of the picture?"

"I think Malia should be the one to outline that. But first, before we get down to business, let's talk pleasure for a moment. I've got the transport all organized for the queen's fete. Two coaches, courtesy of Ezra Chance. I know you girls are in mourning, but the queen is most insistent you come."

"I don't know…" Leilani reached up and fiddled with the mourning cockade in her hair, checking it was still in place

"Come on, Leilani. You know you love it out at the Summer Palace. It's a complete change from in town. It would do you good to escape for a day or two. Ani's absence won't hit you in the face at every turn."

Queen Emma's Summer Palace was a secluded villa an easy coach ride up to the lushly forested Nu'uanu Valley, where the queen had enjoyed retreating with her husband Kamehameha IV and Prince Albert, their adored only son, named after the English king, with Queen Victoria as his godmother.

Emma's Christmas fete was a tradition she'd doggedly continued after the tragic deaths of her husband and son within eighteen months of each other seven years before. A strong and athletic man, Alexander Liholiho had died at age twenty-nine. Although he'd suffered chronic asthma, it was commonly agreed he'd died of a broken heart following four-year-old Prince Albert's death the year before.

"Emma has shown us all how to continue after devastating bereavement," Titus said gently.

"She'll be disappointed if you don't come. She really wants to see you."

"All right, fine. I'll come." She hesitated. "You're obviously coming with us?" Leilani's voice faltered. "Could you bring Aristide with you?"

Titus stopped fiddling with the handle of his coffee cup and looked up in surprise.

"Aristide? I don't see why not. Unless he has something else organized…"

"I just thought it might be nice for him to see a Hawaiian spectacle." Leilani's cheeks reddened, and she spoke her words in a rush. "You know what Emma's fetes are like. Every food and nationality on earth. Dancing, music, crazy horse races. He'd get a glimpse of the old Hawaii, I mean. Before he goes back to California."

Titus shot Malia a conspiratorial look.

"Don't think about it another second, Leilani. I'll make sure he comes. You're right. It would be a great send-off for him."

He reached down to a briefcase he'd lodged at his feet before he'd returned with the coffee.

"Now, let's turn our attention to the plantation business." He pulled a sheaf of papers from the briefcase and put them on the table in front of him.

"A report on the last week, for you. The aftermath, so to speak, of Max's destruction."

Leilani brought her chair closer and looked over his shoulder.

"Where to start? First, I've got to say you'd be proud if you'd seen what Malia achieved while you were away. She sorted some tough stuff out in quick short time."

He looked to Malia, a soft glow in his eyes. "Your turn, sweetheart. You take over from here."

Sweetheart?

Malia glanced to Leilani, whose head had jerked up at the endearment.

Leilani made an approving moue with her mouth. An "oh, I see how the land lies" gesture.

Malia's cheeks warmed. Then she took a deep breath and assumed control.

"We made it very clear to the king that he couldn't have anything to do with Max after he'd humiliated everyone—including him—so badly." She took a sip of her coffee.

"He didn't need persuading—he was livid at the exposure. He called Max in and told him that as long as he held shares in Diamond Sugar, there'd be no water. I believe Max has already packed up and gone. He didn't bother to hang around."

She glanced at Titus.

"But that still left us a bit up in the air, so Titus has been working on a deal to provide water only to us."

She knew her face was turning a deepening rose by the second.

"Lot has verbally agreed to giving Manolo Sugar exclusive rights in perpetuity to the water from his lands. We were just waiting for you to come home to approve it before we all sign it."

She spread her arms wide. "So… taa-daa. No more headaches over water. And you don't have to marry the wrong man to please the king and Ani."

Leilani stared for a few seconds, as if she could hardly believe what she'd heard. Then she clapped her hands together.

"And of course I'll sign it. As soon as we can. Before he changes his mind."

She stood, restless, looking out to the beach, eyes searching the water line. Then she turned back to the coffee tray.

"That's fantastic Malia, you clever thing, you. You don't even need me here. You've managed just fine by yourself."

Malia glanced at Titus. "Not quite by myself, Leilani. This man here has been an absolute boon. We couldn't have done it without him."

Leilani got a wicked look in her eye.

"A talented lawyer is always welcome, but we don't need to go overboard. We don't know him that well yet, do we?"

She broke down in giggles. "I'm teasing, I hope you know."

She turned serious. "Honey came by this morning. She said something about Max selling his share in Diamond. Do you know anything more about that, Titus?"

Titus shuffled the papers in front of him.

"I think we'll know more tomorrow," he said. "I'd prefer to leave it till then to discuss the matter."

***

Leilani. She'd always been the strong, upright one. The sister who took the lead. Who accepted responsibility for the family's future.

As they rode side-by-side back from Titus's Waikiki cottage to downtown, Malia shot furtive glances at her sister. She'd lost weight since the funeral. Maybe the loss had started before Ani died and she hadn't noticed. A gaunt, haunted look shadowed Leilani's fine-boned face. Give her another few weeks like this, and she'd look haggard.

Lani had taken this load upon herself, and Ani had reinforced it. Their brother, Leilani's twin, Kaleo, was more retiring. A gifted swimmer, quick, perceptive and funny. But more of a backroom player. Not one to push himself forward.

And Malia herself? Everyone sidelined her, whether or not they'd meant to, because of her partial blindness. And she'd only come to understand that while Leilani was away in California. In the gap left by her absence, she'd been able to blossom like a sunflower with all the heat and water it required for nourishment.

Malia noted the pain that flashed across her sister's face when she'd lied about Aristide. Sure, she didn't care about him going. And her ingenuous suggestion to include Aristide in the fete? Did she understand her own feelings?

Leilani cared far more than she wanted to admit about Aristide's imminent departure. But here she was, doing it all over again, assuming that she was indispensable. That the family, the sugar business, would fall apart if she wasn't here to manage and direct it.

Malia drew her arms up under her ribs for comfort. They were going to have a big talk, a showdown. But that was for later, when the moment was right.

Thirty-one

"Do you really like him, Malia. I mean. Do you *love* him?"

It was the next day, and they sat in a comfortable open carriage making the journey to the queen's Summer Palace. The air was balmy, the road smooth, and they had no need for the knee rugs so generously provided.

Leilani had to admit that almost as soon as they climbed aboard and she'd escaped the gloomy atmosphere that wrapped around Lot and his home like a cloud, she'd felt the weight on her shoulders lift. She turned to Malia, seated beside her as they passed near Hillebrand's gardens, planted by the German botanist with exotic plants from all around the world, and smiled.

"I guess what I'm asking is, are you serious about him? He can't hide his attraction to you. It shines through the solemn lawyer's front he tries to put up whenever he looks at you…"

Malia shifted in her seat and gazed into the middle distance.

"I think so. I never thought … You know, with my sight as it is, I thought no man would be interested. Let alone one as wonderful as Titus. I'm finding it hard to believe he enjoys my company."

Leilani couldn't swallow for the sadness that lodged in her throat at her sister's words.

"Oh, Malia. I'm so sorry. I've been as guilty as anyone of not giving you your full due. Of maybe treating you too much as someone who 'needed help.'" She broke off. She too gazed out on the lush plantings they were rolling past. "Another of my self-appointed tasks." She grimaced.

"I've always assumed part of my role in the family business was to provide for you, to protect you—and I didn't mind that at all. But that was how I looked at it. I can see now how wrong that was."

She reached out and squeezed Malia's shoulder. Kū, the younger, more energetic of the dogs, jumped up, taking the gesture as a sign something interesting was about to happen, that perhaps they were about to stop and explore all the enticing smells they were passing by.

"Leilani laughed. "Look at him. Always ready for action.'"

She stroked his head. "Nah, Kū, boy. We're going on a long ride to see Queen Emma. We're not doing other stuff today."

She turned back to Malia, her eyes fixed on her face.

"So. Have you talked about marriage?"

Malia's mouth shaped in a shy smile.

"He hasn't proposed, if that's what you're asking. But I think he's got it in mind."

"And if he asks, what will you say?"

Malia glowed with a radiance Leilani had rarely seen in her.

"I'll say yes, of course."

***

They'd quickly left the city wharves far behind and proceeded up a broad ascent on an excellent road to the heart of Oahu, passing gardens overflowing with tropical creepers and fruit and flowers of every description. Cottage owners had complemented native species like breadfruit and coconut with many imported varieties—mangoes, bananas, custard apples, papayas, limes and figs.

At its start the valley took a wide and gentle climb, and the gardens were neatly fenced. But after it crossed the Nu'uanu Stream the slope steepened, and the valley narrowed. Taro beds, dug into plots of mud and water, replaced the picturesque cottages and flower gardens. Beyond the taro were the cemeteries and then the Royal Mausoleum where the Kamehameha kings—including Emma's husband and son—lay.

They fell silent as their journey continued, absorbed as they always were by the lush magnificence of this valley, the heartland where the Kamehameha dynasty established itself in the last of seven decisive battles fought by Kamehameha I in the late 18th century.

"I wonder what Aristide is making of these views." Leilani was musing to herself as much as speaking to Malia, but her sister caught her words.

"I imagine he's overawed, just as we are. But I'm sure you can tell him about it all later, if Titus hasn't already explained."

Malia shot her a quick smile.

Emma's house was a mile from the mausoleum. Beyond it the road narrowed further, and the terrain became more wild and rugged. Kamehameha I had won the title of sole ruler of all the islands in these impregnable mountains. O' Kaiana, one of Kamehameha's last rivals, fell after disputing every boulder and crevasse with club and spear, finally driven off the Pali, the cliff, a sheer precipice where hundreds of warriors died with their chief.

Leilani shivered, even though the day was still hot. "You can feel it in the air, can't you? Blood spilt on sacred ground?"

Malia nodded.

"I'm glad we don't have to fight like that today."

Malia laughed.

***

They'd descended from their comfortable carriage, glad to stretch their legs after the ride.

They'd barely time to follow a servant to their accommodation before Her Royal Highness The Dowager Queen appeared at their sides.

"Leilani! Malia! I am so happy you came! The fete would not be the same without you!"

She took each of them by an arm and strode out with them into the front garden.

"I'm going to be riding tomorrow, and Leilani, I want you to join me."

The queen was famed as a master equestrian.

"I won't take no for an answer," she said with a determined smile. "Now. I want you to take me to your menfolk. Where are they?"

Our menfolk? Does she know something I don't?

Before Leilani had time to consider the question, Titus and Aristide pulled up in a topless gig drawn by a strapping white horse, spraying dust and gravel as they halted, their faces flushed with the exhilaration of the ride.

Queen Emma stayed lodged between Leilani and Malia, squeezing their arms in excitement.

"I knew we'd timed it right."

Titus jumped to the ground, made a courteous bow, and stepped forward to take the dowager queen's hand and kiss it.

"Mr. Cooke! Wonderful to see you again. And who is your friend? Please introduce me."

She cast a mischievous glance toward Malia.

She knows full well who Aristide is, and she's enjoying this.

Leilani slipped alongside Malia to whisper in her ear.

"She's enjoying this. She already knows about you and Titus, too. I can tell."

"Mr. Aristide Laurent. He's an acquaintance of Leilani's brother, Kaleo, from San Francisco. Here for a short visit. We wanted him to see the jewel in Oahu's crown before he returns home."

The queen gave him an almost coquettish smile as she stretched out her hand for Aristide to kiss.

"Kaleo is as treasured in our hearts as his sister, so welcome, Mr. Laurent. I hope you find something of interest."

"Oh I already have, Your Highness. Titus has been sharing the history on the way up here. It's overwhelmingly beautiful."

He turned to look at Leilani and made a slight bow in her direction.

"I feel very privileged to be included."

"I'll get someone to show you to your rooms. You may like to take a breather before dinner. There's a drawing room set aside for your use, with beverages provided. The chamberlain will show you."

A majordomo appeared at her elbow, and led them away.

Now how deftly managed was that?

Leilani exchanged a knowing look with Titus and they both laughed.

***

An hour later, refreshed and rested, they met up again in the drawing room for drinks.

"Leilani, before we get carried away, I've got some news. It just came in today. I think you'll be pleased."

Titus sat at a round table in the middle of the room.

"Before we get onto that, Titus. Thank you for pushing me into coming. I'm already feeling better for being out of the palace and downtown. I don't know which is the more vexing."

Leilani grinned at him. "I hate to say it, but you did know best. Now, what's this news?

Titus glanced briefly to Aristide.

"We had a communication from Senator de Vile this morning."

He caught a scowl flitting across her eager countenance.

"No, don't be like that. I told you. Good news. He's bought Max's share. I imagine de Vile drove a tough deal, and I don't feel in the least bit sorry for Max if he did. He's also got a novel idea for how he wants to let go of those shares."

Leilani sat waiting. "I'm listening. Go on."

"He's disposing of his holding in thirds. He'll give a third to the Cleveland estate. I'm not sure whether this will be to Gerald, or directly to Honey. He'll keep one third for himself. And he proposes to give one third to Manolo Sugar in return for a deal to share in the water rights in perpetuity."

He drew in a deep breath and held on to it.

Leilani sat fixed on the edge of her seat, staring at him, blank-faced.

"He what?"

"He's bartering a share in Diamond for water rights. He'll retain a controlling share in Diamond with the shares he already owns. But you'll have an overall controlling interest in the water dispersal. If you agree, I'll frame the deeds we draw up accordingly."

"But why … Why would he do that?"

"He recognizes it's the only way Diamond will increase production on that plantation. They have other lands, as you know, so it's not as if it is critical to their long-term survival. I suspect it is also his way of extending the olive branch. You now have to decide whether you can cooperate with him in business. I want to remind you that his offer gives you more than a share in the plantation. It includes ownership of shipping and refining as well—so it significantly increases your overall reach as a company."

She stared at Aristide.

"Is this your doing? Is this what you were talking to him about when you met up with him before you came here?"

Her voice sounded almost accusing.

He put up his hands in a mock gesture of seeking cover and took a step back.

"Hey, hey, hey. Easy! I didn't presume to get into details. I just wanted to see where there were possibilities for better understanding."

He glanced at Titus, then back at her again, and shrugged.

"It seems as if the senator has decided there are such opportunities. Nothing to do with me."

Thirty-two

The fete proper began early the next morning with a formal prayer and blessing from the cathedral rector and the fluid, graceful dance of the *hula ʻauana* accompanied by local guitars celebrating secular life—families and love, nature and oral history. Once outlawed by the earliest Calvinist missionaries as indecent, the hula was making a stealthy comeback as the heartbeat and poetry of Hawaiian culture.

Leilani still felt awkward around Aristide. They hadn't regained the easy intimacy they'd enjoyed in California. She supposed they never would, and it saddened her. But she resigned herself to leaving Titus and Aristide to fossick around, following up their interests while she and Malia went their own way.

They drifted past stalls laden with Christmas ornaments and wreaths, some handmade from local materials—shells, pinecones, dried seaweed dipped in white gold and red paint—and handiwork from the church wives' sewing circle: tiny stuffed owls and pigs, gold-braided angels with tissue-paper wings, patchwork cushion covers and quilts

There were home preserves in jewel-like colors—ruby strawberry jam, saffron quince, passionfruit sauce the hue of garnets and fresh fruit of all types, limes, bananas and figs.

In the food market they found pails of purple poi, the popular taro paste that was a staple food for village people. Chinese merchants offered up roast pork and dumplings, pickled vegetables and candied ginger. The fish stall overflowed with fresh fish from every part of the Oahu coast—flying fish and ocean mullet, squid, bonita and dolphin and myriad shellfish and sea mosses the villagers liked to use as relish for poi.

And awa, the root brought on the first canoes to beach here a thousand years ago, made into a relaxing drink similar to Fijian kava.

And wine. She thought of Aristide when she saw the wine. They got talking to the winemaker, who explained he was a great-grandson of the first Hawaiian winemaker, a Spaniard named Don Francisco de Paula Marin, who'd jumped ship in Honolulu and never returned to Alto California. They tasted a drop and found it definitely moreish.

"I hope Aristide finds this one," Leilani said, turning to Malia. "I'm sure he'd be interested."

"Why don't we find him and tell him?"

Malia had a cheeky look on her face.

"No. We don't need to do that. He can find it himself."

Leilani turned so Malia wouldn't see the burn flushing her face and saw a familiar object on a nearby stall. "Oh, look at those," she said, grateful for the distraction. "I want to see those."

The venerable ladies who were looking after the stall were doing a roaring business. Piled high on the table in front of them were mourning cockades in black, white, red and gold and various shapes and designs.

Plaited rosettes with button centers, shoulder brooches with colorful ribbon strings, or hat cockades similar to the one she had worn to Ani's funeral.

They all carried a small parchment label in elegant calligraphy giving the briefest details of Ani's life; her name, birth and death dates and a phrase in Hawaiian: *Ua Mau ke Ea o ka Āina I ko Pono.*

The life of the land is perpetuated in righteousness.

It was a famous saying from a speech by Kamehameha III, and a line of people, old and young, men and women, were lining up to buy. Leilani's hand flew to her throat, and she pushed back her tears.

"Look! Look, Malia."

She drew her sister close.

"Look what the queen or someone close to her has organized. They've remembered Ani. If she knew, I think she'd consider all her suffering worthwhile."

As they walked on, she kept hold of Malia's arm and they walked close. She was almost whispering in Malia's ear.

"I've been thinking about our Ani a lot this last week. You know her life was one of service to others—particularly us and the king's family. From the day Archie gave Matthew Lilolilo to our mother and drafted her in to look after us when Abbie died—from that day, she served those who she had the most reason to despise.

"She missed out on her chance at love because of our mother. And then she raised the brats begotten of an ill-fated marriage that caused her pain. That's bravery under fire. That's the action of a soldier."

Malia paused and whispered back. "I think she loved us. I hope she knew we loved her back. But you're right. It's a tough thing to live with."

"So much damage created by people trying to run other people's lives," said Leilani with a hint of regret.

"And I had a very narrow escape."

***

Aristide and Titus stood with Malia on the sideline and watched, entranced, as the queen and Leilani joined thirty or more other women in a flamboyant helter-skelter horseback ride, the traditional event known as Pa'u. They rode astride their steeds at breakneck

151

speed, executing tight turns and feinting and bluffing to force other riders to give way.

Dressed in long flowing skirts that trailed to the ground, their horses bedecked in flower garlands, they made a pleasing interlude to the other afternoon events—the men's wrestling and the children chasing a greased piglet. At the end of it all, it surprised no one when the crown for Pa'u rider of the day went to the queen.

Titus and Aristide wandered away from the Pa'u ring to where a series of fine singing groups competed for crowd applause. One haunting melody in particular caught their attention.

"'*Adios Ke Aloha,* '" said Titus. "'Goodbye, My Love.'"

Aristide winced. "More appropriate than I'd like."

Titus smiled in sympathy, as they listened in reflective silence.

"It's a popular lover's farewell song—as you can tell from the 'Adios,' it's influenced by Mexican cowboys who came here in the 1830s to teach the local *paniolas*—the Hawaiian cattle herders—how to rope wild bulls."

He gave Aristide another wry grin. "Here's how the last verse goes…"
'One kiss
As cool as a dew drop, will do
O belle of the ice-cold mist
Here I am, your lover
Returning empty handed.'"

Titus clapped Aristide on the back as they returned to the house to change for dinner.

"You got an insight into Hawaiian culture today, that's for sure," he said.

"Not too many visitors get to go to Queen Emma's Christmas Fete. Or here the Royal Glee Club singing *Adios Ke Aloha.*"

***

As they clattered into the stables at the end of the Pa'u, Leilani slipped off her bay mare and approached the queen, still seated in her saddle. She patted the side of the queen's glistening black gelding.

"Thank you for pushing me into that. It was tremendous fun, Your Majesty. You gave us all a great contest."

The queen threw back her head and laughed.

She's only thirty-four, thought Leilani. *Ten years older than me. But what she's had to endure…*

"Your Majesty, I wonder if I could have a private word. I thank you sincerely for the tribute you've given to Ani today. I wouldn't have missed it. But there is still something I'd like to discuss with you, if you have a moment. It won't take long."

The queen motioned she was ready to dismount and Leilani hurriedly stepped back.

"Happy to help in any way I can, Leilani. Let's get freshened up and changed. I'll see you in my sitting room in forty minutes."

Thirty-three

"Your Majesty." Leilani licked her lips nervously. Suddenly her mouth felt parched.

"Please forgive me for intruding on your very busy life, and especially at a time like this, with the fete and everything…"

Emma waved her hand as if the swarming crowds, the myriad demands on her time, were nothing of consequence.

"That's what we have excellent staff for. They take care of all that. I am interested in what you have to say. That is my sole focus at this moment."

Leilani shifted in her chair. Her heart was pounding.

What if the queen thought her impertinent?

"Your Majesty, I wanted to talk to you about the Royal House. I am sure you know that through my mother's husband Matthew Lilolilo, I had a minor link to the Kamehameha line?"

Emma tilted her head like a bird expecting to be fed.

"Of course. That's well known, Leilani. What of it?"

Her voice was gentle, and Leilani had a deep sense that what she was going to say next would not be a surprise.

"I've become aware, just in recent months, of things I have never known about my parentage until now. I suspect you've already heard of this, if you haven't known it for many years."

Emma smiled softly.

"I think it would be a good idea if you tell me what you are referring to, Leilani. No guessing games."

Leilani cleared her throat and took a deep breath. She'd hardly discussed this with anyone. Aristide, her brother and Malia, Elizabeth Wenderhoven… No one else. It was her deepest personal secret.

"When I was in San Francisco this summer, I discovered what we—my twin brother Kaleo and I—had been told a false story about our birth. Our father was not Matthew Lilolilo, but another man, a sea captain who is now a powerful Washington senator, Hector de Vile. Truth is, our grandfather Archie Arnold also deceived Senator de Vile. Only a very few people—my darling Ani among them—knew what happened, and most of them are now dead."

Emma nodded and let out a deep sigh.

"I had heard rumors to that effect."

"It's all in the past as to why and how. But it's been on my heart so much over the past month, because it's slowly dawned on me that part of the reason the king was keen to push my marriage to Max Moeller was because of the possibility of introducing new heirs into the Kamehameha line. I was focused on the sugar plantation, on the water, when this all started out. On securing our family fortunes. That was my main concern.

"But now… Now I feel I've been presented to King Lot under false pretenses. And it is just too tender a subject for me to raise with him directly."

She jumped to her feet, wringing her hands, alive now with urgent energy.

"I know you'll understand, Your Majesty. Ani loved Lilolilo. She hoped to marry him, and then she lost out when Archie forced my mother to marry him instead. Ani told us the story last week, just before she died, and I'm so glad she did.

"My sister—my half-sister now, Malia—we always thought her childhood blindness would hamper her from living a normal life, but we've been wrong. So wrong about that. She's brilliantly capable of taking a lead, and it's highly likely she'll be engaged to Titus Cooke within a few months.

"And she…" She spun around, her eyes blazing, she knew, and gazed at the queen as if willing her to understand. "She's Matthew Lilolilo's daughter. No doubt."

Queen Emma looked at her in silence, a soft smile on her lips.

Leilani dropped back down into her chair, wringing her hands in her lap.

"Queen Emma, I know you and the king have a very close friendship. I know as the bereaved mother of the last Hawaiian heir you have a better understanding than anyone of what all this means. And I am begging you, please, to speak to the king on our behalf, Malia's and mine. Explain all of this. And when the time is appropriate, ask him for his blessing on Malia and Titus. There may yet be a Kamehameha heir, distant though he or she may be."

There was a long silence. Queen Emma drew her linked hands up in front of her face, and gazed at Leilani.

"My goodness, Leilani. That was quite some speech." She gave a tinkling laugh.

"And you are quite correct in your understanding, my dear. In the innermost circles we've known for some time. What you say is correct. It's convenient for Lot to leave the myth undisturbed. Archie rooted it so strongly, so why upset the apple cart. That's his view.

"Can I ask, though, where does this leave you? What do you intend, for your life? You're only getting started. There will be other opportunities—many other opportunities—for you, here in Hawaii."

Leilani's chest tightened, and her face grew hot.

"I have behaved very badly over all of this. I have refused to have anything to do with my father, because I thought it was him behind the attacks on Manolo Sugar which I now know, ironically, were Max's work. The senator has been generous enough to offer us— Manolo Sugar—a business partnership over the plantations and the water rights business. I want to go back to California and mend fences. See what opportunities exist for us to expand our business there. I can see Malia can manage the island end of it, especially with Titus at her side."

The queen's eyes sparkled and the corners of her mouth curled up teasingly.

"And all of this had got nothing at all to do with a certain rather debonair French man?"

She tilted her fingers in front of her mouth again and smiled over the top of them.

"Mr. Laurent, I believe was his name? When I met him today I did wonder what on earth was wrong with you if you were going to let him get away on you."

And she broke into gay laughter.

"I'm being a naughty tease, Leilani. Don't let that bother you. But seriously. Is this what you want?"

Leilani took a deep breath. "I want the king to approve the agreement Titus is drawing up for shared water rights between Diamond and us—something I know was always his first choice. He wants to keep all his major business concerns happy. If it comes to fruition, I wish him to give his kingly approval to the union of my sister and Mr. Cooke. And I'd truly appreciate his blessing on my return to California to look after Hawaiian sugar interests there."

She placed her palms flat together in a gesture of prayer.

"If you could get the king to see, to agree to all this, I'd be grateful my whole life."

"And that's all?" The queen still had a cheeky question in her eyes.

Leilani looked down at her hands, suddenly shy of meeting Emma's gaze head-on.

"No. Not all. I still have to find a way back into Mr. Laurent's heart. We were very close once… but that feels like a long time ago. I hope I haven't done irreparable damage to something I've realized is precious to me."

Thirty-four

The hordes had departed, the stalls and the merchandise all packed up and taken away, and the horses groomed, fed and stabled.

A much smaller "family" group gathered in Queen Emma's dining room for her Christmas fete thanksgiving dinner. It was the dowager's way of unwinding after a tumultuous day, enjoying a convivial family atmosphere that was lacking since the deaths of her husband and son, and everyone at the table understood it. They were all here in tribute to her.

And Aristide had gone. That was the first thing Leilani saw as she entered the room and spied Malia already seated, an empty chair beside her. She wended her way across the finely woven mats to her sister and tapped the chair back.

"Are you saving this for me?"

"Indeed, I am, dear Sis. The chaps had to go back to town on urgent business."

Leilani's chest and arms felt suddenly tight. Until just this moment, she hadn't realized how much she'd banked on having a chance to talk to Aristide tonight. To melt the ice that had formed between them. To find a way back into his affections, if she could.

She'd taken special care with her appearance, adding a touch of artificial color to her cheeks, dressing her hair with extra care so it framed her face and enhanced her dark eyes. She fiddled with the stiff white napkin that lay beside the silver knife at her place setting and fought to hide her disappointment.

"Something to do with our ongoing business?" she asked. She wanted to appear ever-so-casual, but even to her own ears, her speech sounded strangled.

Malia looked up sharply, picking up, Leilani was certain, on the strain in her voice. Her sister never missed a beat in the things left unsaid.

"Yes. He wants to get it finalized as quickly as he can."

Leilani's eyes flicked toward the head of the table, where the queen sat, regal in an imperial purple gown, one of the "Ani cockades" set above dangling black onyx earrings.

She leaned in to her sister. "I had a reassuring talk with the queen this afternoon. I'll fill you in later."

Malia raised her eyebrows.

"Really? How fascinating."

Leilani glanced around her. The room oozed wealth and high status, from the padded mahogany chairs, to the antique cabinet against the wall filled with precious china, to the liveried servants at the ready around the room.

A commanding chandelier sparkled light onto the dazzling white linen-clad table, reflecting off the crystal wineglasses and silver cutlery.

A dramatic festive centerpiece in red and white flora graced the table—red *ōhi'a lehua*, white ginger, pikake—the sweet-smelling Arabian jasmine which had quickly become a favorite for leis, all threaded with golden angels, their gossamer-light muslin wings looking like they were about to take flight for the heavens. All wreathed in a black velvet base.

"The queen does everything so well," she breathed to Malia. "She's the most remarkable woman."

She looked around her. The guests were a predictable crew of House of Nobles members and privy councillors like Ezra Chance and David Kinau and their wives. There was John Dominis and wife Lydia and his mother Mary. And there was—no—surely not. Honey Cleveland.

"What's she doing here?" she asked Malia. She couldn't suppress the slightly sour note to the question.

Malia looked up.

"Who? Oh, you mean Honey? Oh, I think she's leaving Hawaii too, soon. She wanted to pay her respects to the queen before she did. Why? You don't object?"

Malia's voice was disbelieving.

She leaned over and whispered. "You're not jealous, are you?"

Leilani pulled back as if she'd touched a hot stove.

"Jealous? Of course not."

Malia started laughing. "You are, you silly mule. Talk to her. You'll find out."

She'd been looking forward to this dinner, usually served up like an early Christmas feast with all the traditional trimmings—roast turkey and vegetables, barbecued pork and greens, shellfish from one of the vendor's earlier today—but she'd been wrong.

She wasn't hungry at all. A grueling pain started low in her stomach, and suddenly she didn't want to be here, pretending to be convivial. All she really wanted to do was crawl into bed and cry.

She waited until the natural pause between courses. The guests stood. The men went outside to smoke. Ladies excused themselves to use the bathroom. And Leilani hurried to where Honey sat, momentarily unattended by the good-looking city banker Malia had let drop was her escort for the night.

"Honey! Nice to see you."

Leilani cringed inside. She was the most dreadful actress. Would anybody believe she was genuine?

Honey looked up and grinned. She was ready to accept her friendliness on face value.

"Leilani! I've heard you made an impressive display on the Pa'u course this afternoon. Nearly as good as the queen, I was told. You dark horse you!" She giggled. "I know. Terrible pun. Forgive me. I couldn't resist."

Despite herself, Leilani warmed to the young heiress.

"You've heard the news? About de Vile?"

"I have. Still waiting to hear if the shares are going to be in my father's name or mine."

She crunched up her mouth as if she tasted something unpleasant.

"I've told Titus if he can do it, make it direct to me, or it might get gambled away like the last lot."

"Titus again. Is he handling your business too?"

"He seems to have the open line to the senator…"

"And Malia says you're going back home soon, anyway."

"Yes. Leaving on Christmas Eve."

"On the Moses Taylor?"

"Yes. Why?"

The horrible sick pain in Leilani's gut returned in a whoosh.

"That's the same steamer Aristide is going back on. Isn't it?"

Honey shrugged. "Quite possibly." She stopped twiddling with the stem of her wineglass and stared at Leilani.

"Oh, my goodness. You don't think… You do… You think I've got an amour going with Aristide."

She dissolved into peals of laughter. Several people around them glanced their way, curious to share the joke.

Irritation welled up, briefly masking the stomach ache, as Leilani sat staring at the tablecloth, turning red.

"No. Nothing like that." Her voice was feeble and unconvincing.

"Oh, my goodness, girl. Get up." She took Leilani by the elbow. "We're taking a walk, and I'm telling you a few home truths noone might have mentioned to you before."

Despite herself, Leilani rose and allowed Honey to lead her into the garden.

"This reminds me of my visit to the glowworm cave with Aristide. It had much the same purpose."

"I've got no idea what you mean."

"Listen, Leilani. I was never interested in Aristide. He's too poor. I need someone who can keep me in the style I want." She gave a nonchalant shrug.

"Just being honest. And anyway, he's madly in love with you. That was obvious from the first day I met him."

Leilani stared at the pretty rosebud mouth, which kept on moving up and down. She couldn't hear a darn thing. Her head was still buzzing on the words "madly in love."

She stopped walking. Grabbed Honey's elbow. "Stop. Stop walking. Stop talking.

"Take a deep breath. Now. Both of us. A deep breath."

Honey looked amused but followed suit.

A brilliant sky set the trees in dark silhouette. The air was cool. She took a few more fresh, expansive breaths.

"Good. Now say that again. What you just said before. About Aristide."

Arrgh. She sounded like she was pleading.

Honey gazed at her, momentarily puzzled. Then she gave a broad smile.

"Oh… oh, I see."

She glanced around to see if anyone else was nearby, but they were alone.

She leaned in. In an accented French whisper she repeated: "Aristide is madly in love. With you. Not me. You."

"That's what I thought you said. Just wanted to make sure."

"You silly cow. Why do you think he came all the way to Hawaii? It wasn't to see volcanoes. It wasn't because he's in love with Titus. Mercy on my soul. I only took him off to the grotto to make Max jealous. And thanks to you as much as anyone, I'm spared that fate now. I really owe you one."

She grinned. "Consider my debt paid. Shall we get dessert now? I'm looking forward to ice cream."

She turned to go back inside, but Leilani grabbed her arm again.

"Hold on a minute. Just one more thing."

Honey stopped. "What?"

"You won't mind if I join you on the Moses Taylor? But no telling anyone. Understood? This one's our secret."

Thirty-five

The engineers were shoveling coal, and the boilers firing up as Aristide boarded the Moses Taylor, the North Pacific Transportation Company's steamship, a small leather suitcase swinging from one arm. He'd arrived early, alone, and traveling light, as intended. He'd told Titus he wanted no fuss about his San Francisco departure.

He preferred to slip out of Honolulu without fanfare, just the way he'd arrived. Heavens knew, nothing had turned out the way he'd hoped, and this return voyage was his time to brace himself, to accept failure and prepare for a new season.

And there would be a new season. His Vino d'Oro wines were gaining acclaim in New York. He expected by the time he docked in the Bay his sister Madeleine and her grazier husband Caleb would be celebrating the birth of their first child.

One of the people he most looked forward to meeting after he stepped off the Moses Taylor was his new godson—or goddaughter.

He got his first inkling that his departure would not be as quiet as he'd planned when the women from the Port Auxiliary Committee arrived to set up a lei station for departing passengers.

The town was introducing Steamer Days, when all San Francisco-bound passengers—resident or tourist—were farewelled with a fragrant farewell lei and music from the Royal Hawaiian Band to ensure they felt loved, valued, and encouraged to return.

He'd stowed his luggage in his shared cabin and gone back up on deck just in time to hear the band striking up a familiar song. It was the one from the Queen's fete, "*Adios Ke Aloha,*" "Goodbye My Love." Written by a gifted royal musician who'd died at age twenty-two.

Aristide laughed under his breath.

Life does go around in strange circles.

On the dock a substantial crowd was gathering.

The Moses Taylor could take three hundred passengers, and although he had no idea how heavily booked the ship might be, he guessed every one of the folk boarding except him had friends and family keen to see them off.

The ship wasn't due to leave for another two hours, and food vendors and street hustlers weren't missing the opportunity to sell to a captive audience.

Above the din he imagined he heard someone call his name. He stared out into the colorful crowd and saw an arm, waving a Hawaiian flag. Malia's arm.

He looked again. Titus was standing to her left, his arm around her waist, while on his other side stood Honey Cleveland. When his lawyer friend saw they'd managed to attract his attention, he beckoned him to join them.

"Come down here!" Titus bawled like a fairground barker above the din. Aristide scowled and stood his ground.

Titus gestured again.

"Down here now!"

Honey and Malia were laughing and nodding in agreement.

Aristide slipped down the gangplank and went over to them.

"What are you doing? Didn't I say I didn't want a fuss?"

He was laughing, and hugging Malia and Honey as he spoke. He clapped Titus on the shoulder. "Never trust a lawyer."

Honey stepped in close.

"We can't leave without a tiny bit of ceremony. We must get our leis, to remind us of Hawaii's beauty for a start. They'll keep for days, a nice reminder. And I don't want my traveling companion to be a stick-in-the-mud. That doesn't fit your debonair reputation at all."

Aristide laughed. "Debonair? I hardly think so. And besides, where's your luggage?"

As he spoke a muscular wharf hand, his bare arms gleaming with sweat, appeared at Honey's elbow, dragging a trolley piled with a tottering six-high stack of steamer trunks and hat boxes.

"Where do you want these, ma'am?"

"Ha!" Aristide cried in laughter. "Now I see why you lured me down here. Looking for willing slaves, are you?"

She turned to the porter. "Be with you in a moment. It's Cabin Number 200. With a porthole on the starboard side."

She turned back to Aristide. "You're coming with me. We're getting our leis before we board."

She elbowed him jocularly over to a table set back from the water's edge, mounded high with sweet-smelling pink and white blossoms. The women who were unhurriedly dispensing the fragrant leis were themselves crowned with a circlet of white flowers in their hair.

As Aristide presented himself, a full-figured, grandmotherly woman with a flower garland in hand paused before him.

"Aloha," she said. "And safe traveling." She draped the sweet-smelling flowers around his neck with calm grace. He felt the cool dampness of the petals against his neck, and drank in the serenity she radiated amid the surrounding buzz.

Aristide turned to Honey and smiled.

"This was a good idea." He dipped his chin and nuzzled the flowers, smelling of jasmine and a candied, slightly metallic tuberose.

"A very good idea. Thanks for calling me out on being a spoilsport."

They turned to spot Malia, flag still aloft, and made their way back to find the steamship porter patiently awaiting Honey's return.

"I'm going to accompany this good man on board. See you in a while." Honey flipped her fingers at him and disappeared with the trolley.

Aristide turned back, preparing to make his final farewell to Titus.

Except Titus wasn't there. Standing in his place was the woman he'd never forget, with a pink and white lei around her neck.

"Leilani!" Her name jumped unbidden out of his throat. "What… What are you doing here?"

She was as still as a windless lake at dawn. Not a ripple penetrated her surface. She looked into his eyes and said, "I'm here to make friends."

"Make friends?"

His heart stalled, poised between hope and despair.

"I'm sorry, I don't understand. Don't you already have plenty of friends?"

It sounded stupid, he knew it. But what was she talking about? *Friends?* His head seemed to echo with the word, as if she'd spoken in an unfamiliar language.

Leilani stepped closer and took his right wrist gently between her thumb and index finger. Her touch was light, and as she moved, he caught a whiff of her fresh green perfume, the one that smelled of ferns and waterfalls.

"But *we're* not friends, Aristide. I want for us to be friends again. And more than friends, if you so wish it."

He felt as if his mind was operating at half speed, barely able to process her words, let alone make sense of them.

"I want to make up for my horrible behavior, Aristide. I want to tell you I so admire the courageous way you came here, searching me out, taking the risk of being rejected. You are a true gallant. And I was a barbarian."

She took hold of his left wrist and searched his eyes. "I want to be more like you."

They stood like that for long seconds; he had no idea how long. Time lost its meaning. The noise on the wharf faded. There were two people in the world, him and this darling woman who held him in loving captivity.

"I want to be valiant, like you. To risk humiliation to say what I truly feel. And to hope with all my heart that we can get back to where I might hold a small place in your affections."

She dropped her hands from his wrists then. He stepped closer, so the buttons of his jacket brushed the front of her dress.

He took her face gently in both hands and ran his fingers down her cheekbones, his touch so light it was hardly there, and yet … He felt her shiver, and tears welled up in her eyes. She felt something too.

"Lani Manolo. I have never for one moment stopped loving you." He gave a quick gulp of laughter and looked tenderly into her wet eyes. "Even when you were at your worst. And I do agree, your worst was pretty awful."

She hiccupped a laugh then and placed her hands over the top of his.

"There is hope for us? We can build a bridge? A bridge back to each other? And then I hope you will help me build a bridge to my father. You already know a lot more about how to do that than I do."

She turned away, her eyes searching for Titus and Malia in the swirling crowds.

The Kings' Band struck up the first chords of *Auld Lang Syne*, and Aristide glanced to Lani's feet, where a moderate-sized steamer trunk sat.

At the same moment, Titus and Malia reappeared.

"Well, you two. Time to board, I think. After all this fuss I wouldn't like to see one of you left behind." Titus gave them a generous grin.

Malia reached in and hugged them both. "Don't worry about anything here, we've got it."

She looked to Aristide. "Lani's mentioned she'd got a lot of making up to do, so we won't interrupt you any longer."

"Mon Dieu! You both knew too! Everyone except me, it seems, was in on the secret."

He turned to Leilani and gave her side a playful squeeze.

"You've some explaining to do," he laughed.

"Yep! And we've got two weeks at sea to get started."

Epilogue

"We did it." Mrs. Aristide Laurent looked lovingly up at her husband-of-one-day and laughed. "We broke Pele's curse."

The French vintner with the adorable black lock of hair that flopped over one eye frowned down at her drowsily.

"Pele's curse? That's the Hawaiian god of volcanoes?"

"Don't you remember? When we walked the beach before I went back to Honolulu last year? I told you the story of Ōhi'a and Lehua."

"Ohhh yes, I remember now. The jealous god who wanted to keep the two lovers apart."

"I feel as if something like that happened to us. Only it wasn't a jealous god. More of a generational curse. We suffered the consequences of the wrong actions of others."

"That's one way to see it, I suppose. But thankfully, we're free to fulfil our destiny."

From their carved four-poster bed they could see out through the hacienda's wide-silled windows to sloping rows of Zinfandel grapes, the new growth a vibrant green in the shafted early morning light.

They occupied a comfortable old Spanish villa on the Vino d'Oro estate close to Caleb and Madeleine's ranch, and if they'd been looking out, they'd have seen the hawk circling lazily overhead, waiting to breakfast on the smaller birds darting in and out of Vino d'Oro's soon-to-bloom vines.

However, Aristide and Leilani weren't watching for birds. They had eyes only for each other.

Aristide stroked a hand down his wife's radiant face. "I knew it the first night we met, do you realize? I knew we were destined to be together. It just took the universe a while to catch up."

He brushed her hair off her face with infinite tenderness.

"The most wonderful thing in the world can happen today, and every day from now on…"

He leaned over her.

"I can kiss my wife. How are you this morning, Mademoiselle Laurent?"

They'd wed in a small greenery-festooned local church, followed by an outdoor lunch on tables set amidst the grapes, surrounded by the family that loved them.

For Leilani soon saw that with Aristide at her side, she'd acquired a populous and loving Golden State family, beginning with the woman who'd helped her understand and accept much of what had gone before, Elizabeth Westerhoven.

When she arrived back in San Francisco six months ago, the rich widow, known affectionately as "the Countess" to many because of her dead husband's links to Austrian nobility, insisted she stay with her in her Nob Hill villa for as long as she liked.

"However long it takes, Leilani. You go about your business. I always felt sad about not being there when you were little, as Abigail would have wished. Now's my chance to make up for it. And it's wonderful to have a daughter after all the years I've spent alone."

Elizabeth was like the cherished mother she'd never known, a remarkable complement to Ani's stern rigor, familiar with Hawaiian conventions but also able to give the wisest advice about the California scene and Hector de Vile, whom she'd known long ago.

With her careful guidance and Aristide's loving support, Leilani had begun the process of reconciliation with the father she'd so resented. They'd come so far that Senator Hector de Vile had given her away, proudly offering his arm as they entered the church under a shower of rose petals thrown by her attendants, who'd then followed in her footsteps with much gaiety.

Aristide's sister Madeleine, a proud new mother of baby son Jean Claude, and the matron of honor, led the charge, followed by bridesmaids Honey and Malia on her heels.

In the last six months Honey had become a good friend. It hadn't been a big surprise to learn she passionately supported the nascent women's suffrage movement that was beginning to demand social change. Leilani had come to value Honey's determination to "pull back the velvet curtain," as she described it, and extend women's rights and freedom.

At the head of the nave, best man Titus Cooke waited with Aristide.

As she made her way forward, Leilani was aware of the cohort she was passing through. All of the Russell brothers—Sir John and his wife Pania, with son Robert, named after John's father and just over a year old. John's other brothers—Sebastian and his wife Isabella, and the youngest, Nathan, with wife Gracie, with their daughter Minette and toddler George.

All there as a tribute to Aristide and his work in building d'Oro's growing international reputation. On the other side, there was Madeleine's husband Caleb's family—his mother, the regal Dona Valentina, twin brothers Lucas and Mateo, his sister Josefa and her husband Santiago with baby Julius, and Santiago's mother, Benecio. Caleb was a partner in d'Oro and engrossed in Aristide's instruction on viticulture.

Of course Leilani's twin brother Kaleo was quietly present, along with his colleagues at Pike Consulting—Will Davenport and office manager Sarah. Last year she'd thought Kaleo might have a romantic interest in Sarah, but if he did she'd seen no evidence it was going anywhere since she'd been back from Honolulu.

Leilani was especially pleased to see Occidental Hotel service manager Sam Morley and his son Teddy near the front, because she'd made a point of specially inviting them. She wanted them there to honor Mamie Bilouxie, her friend, and their wife and mother, who'd died last year in a toxic wine scandal.

Now, the morning after the wedding, Leilani smiled into her husband's eyes, luxuriating in the soft comfort of goose down and the sureness of his love.

"Do you think when Teddy's older we might take him on here at d'Oro? Train him up in wine?"

Aristide leaned over and peppered her forehead with light kisses. The errant lock tickled her cheek and she giggled.

"There you go again. Always looking to make life better for someone else."

He rolled onto his back, gathering her in his arms as he did, so she ended up pressed against his chest, looking down into his eyes.

"Did I tell you that's just one of the many things I adore about you? That and the way you are already saying 'we' when it comes to d'Oro."

He stroked down her neck.

"Teddy? Sure… I think 'we' very well could."

THE END

If you enjoyed *Captive Heart* you may also enjoy
Ancient Vendetta, Book 9 in Of Gold & Blood, a
full-length mystery.

A man – or a woman - who desires revenge should dig two graves …

When San Francisco merchant Kaleo Manolo interrupts an attempted street abduction, he finds himself drawn into a dangerous underground conflict where everyone has something to hide and nothing is what it seems.

Sarah Mountier is a brilliant mathematician and heiress to a substantial fortune forced to conceal her true identity from all, including her eye-catching-and principled protector.

But when the blackmailers searching for Sarah turn their sights on Kaleo, she must decide: can she trust her defender enough to tell him who she really is? And after she'd deceived him for so long, will the man she's come to love believe her?

As they work together to confront forces intent on destroying them both, they must decide if risking their lives is worth the price of their freedom.

Ancient Vendetta is scheduled for publication mid 2021.
Get updates on the free preview and pre-orders - and regular free book offers at:
www.jennywheeler.biz/ancient-vendetta-a-san-francisco-mystery/

Enjoy Captive Heart?
You can make a big difference

Reviews are the most powerful tools in my kit when it comes to getting my books noticed. Much as I'd love it, I don't have the budget of a big publisher to buy billboard ads and other national advertising.

But I have the promise of something more powerful—something publishers envy.

And that's a committed and loyal bunch of readers.

Honest reviews of my books help them gain the attention of others who might appreciate them too.

If you've enjoyed Captive Heart, I would be grateful if you could spend a few minutes leaving a review (it can be as short as you like) on the one of the listed book sites.

Post Your Reviews Here:
Goodreads: https://bit.ly/2JXSsik

Thank you very much
Jenny Wheeler

ACKNOWLEDGMENTS

Like most historical fiction authors, it's important to me to tread a delicate path between historical accuracy and fiction, and never more so than in dealing with royal history. It was a fascinating experience to learn more about the Hawaiian monarchy in the mid-19th century, and I have endeavoured to stay true to the facts in describing living people.

However, I admit to one "fudging" of fact and fiction I entered into with eyes wide open, and that's the selection of the farewell love song sung on the Honolulu wharf as the Moses Taylor steamer is due to depart. The historical record indicates *Adios Ke Aloha* probably wasn't written until a few years later that December 1870. The gifted musician who was its creator, Prince William Pitt Leleiohoku II, died in 1877 at the distressingly young age of 22. He wrote most of his beloved and admired songs in the early 1870s.

I wanted to recognize historical fact, while also trusting readers will be happy to let the lines smudge a little to allow us to imagine a poignant wharf scene, and to pay tribute to a remarkable musician whose life was cut tragically short.

Thank you to the wonderfully loyal readers who continue to support my work—and give me feedback on decisions on things like cover and title selection through my newsletter.

Finally, thank you once again to the professional skills of editor

Stephanie Parent in the US, who worked to stiff deadlines with great grace, and Polgarus Studios in Tasmania for getting Captive Heart into shape for sharing with a wider audience. – Jenny Wheeler

ABOUT THE AUTHOR

Jenny Wheeler is the author of the Of Gold & Blood Old California mystery series:

Poisoned Legacy #1.
Brother Betrayed #2.
Double Jeopardy #3.
Tangled Destiny #4 (Christmas novella and Prequel.)
Unbridled Vengeance #5
Hope Redeemed #6
Tainted Fortune Book #7 (September 2020)
Captive Heart – A Hawaiian Christmas Novella
Ancient Vendetta #9
Boxed Set/Book Bundle Of Gold & Blood, Series 1 Books 1 – 3
Boxed Set/ Book Bundle Of Gold & Blood Series 2 Books 1 & 4

Jenny's online home is at jennywheeler.biz or email
Jenny@jennywheeler.biz

You can connect with Jenny on:
Facebook: @JennyWheeler.Biz
Twitter: @Jenny_Biz
Instagram: @jennysbingereading
Pinterest https://www.pinterest.nz/Jennywheelerbooks